Petteril's

Lord Petteril M

Mary Lancaster

Petteril's Portrait

Chapter One

Having paid his dues, Piers Withan, Viscount Petteril, drove his beautifully matched greys through the crossroads tollgate.

Abruptly, the sunny chatter of his assistant, April, who sat beside him in the curricle, turned off like a tap. He did not need to look at her to know she was scowling at him.

"You've gone the wrong way," she barked. "Sign says Sillitrees is straight on, not left. Will we have to pay the toll again?"

"Not yet. We're going to stay the night at Pelton Park."

"What's Pelton Park?"

"The country seat of Sir Peter Haggard."

April sat bolt upright. "What we going there for?"

There was deep suspicion as well as aggression in her voice. Piers sighed but decided to ignore her attitude rather than make a huge issue out of the matter.

"Sir Peter asked me to call in on the way to Sillitrees."

"Why?"

"I daresay we'll find out when we get there."

"Is *she* there?"

"Who?"

"The stepma! Lady 'Aggard."

"Yes, she is."

Piers could feel the tension radiating from her, but at least she didn't try to jump out of the curricle. To discourage any such antics, he urged the horses to a faster pace. But she sat back, gazing straight ahead with a not very convincing air of unconcern.

1

"Mr. Stewart and the baggage going there, too?" she asked.

"Yes, though depending on the available space at Pelton, I might send him on to Sillitrees."

"Good idea," April said generously. "I'll go ahead with him, then, and make sure Sillitrees is in a decent state for you."

"Oh, no," Piers said, imagining the faces of whatever respectable servants remained at Sillitrees when April tried to exert authority. "I suspect I shall need you at Pelton. I understand there has been a bit of an accident."

He risked a glance at her glowering profile. How could anyone look so ridiculously pretty with an expression like that? Curiosity, which he was banking on, warred with continued suspicion in her young, piquant face and old, old eyes.

She turned suddenly, catching his gaze. "What sort of accident?"

"I'm not sure. Haggard's note gave little away, but he doesn't shout for help over nothing."

She searched his face, looking for the lie, which hurt him more than it should. She still didn't trust him fully. "Maybe not," she said grudgingly. "I suppose they got lots of servants."

"I suppose they have."

"They won't know my place."

"*You* don't know your place," he retorted. Actually, neither did he.

He had first encountered her at the lowest point in his life, three months ago, when she had been dressed as a boy and burgling his house in the dead of night. An inauspicious beginning, but one he had never regretted.

"Lady Haggard will look after you," he said unwisely, hoping only to remove the fear from behind her intense blue eyes. It had the opposite effect.

"I don't need looking after!" she spat. "I ain't a child and she ain't my guvnor."

"All the same, you will obey her," Piers said coldly.

He received no reply. When he glanced at her again, her face was mutinous, her body rigid. She was angry and afraid he was going to abandon her with Lady Haggard as he had suggested several times over the weeks of their acquaintance. With his head, he knew this would be the kindest thing he could do for April, but she disagreed.

He drove in silence for more than a mile before, having slowed the horses on a particularly rough stretch of road, he nudged her with his elbow.

"It will be fine," he said.

"It won't," April said through stiff lips.

AN HOUR LATER, THEY drove through the gates of Pelton Park and along a gravel drive to a gracious Queen Anne period manor house. By the time Piers pulled up, stable lads were running toward them to take the horses and the baggage. Even so, April jumped down and reached the horses' heads well in advance.

While she stroked their necks and slipped them pieces of a some-what fluffy carrot extracted from the leather bag at her girdle, Piers stepped down at a more leisurely pace. Over the singing of blackbirds and thrushes, he could hear laughter and many voices drifting on the breeze from the gardens behind the house.

His heart sank. He hoped they were mere morning callers and not house guests. The front door opened, and a gentleman leapt down the steps.

"Haggs," April muttered to Piers, releasing the horses to the care of the stable lads.

Haggs was what Piers called his friend. It was certainly not April's place to refer to him so, but she had to speak quickly before he was up-on them, and Piers was grateful for the information.

"No idea who she is," April added as a lady descended the front steps at a more dignified pace.

"Withy! Delighted," Sir Peter Haggard exclaimed, grasping his hand and wringing it. His harsh, ugly-attractive features meshed with his familiar voice and Piers grinned, thumping him on the shoulder.

Haggs turned immediately to the lady who had followed him out of the house. She was, Piers guessed, somewhere in her early thirties, with dark hair and eyes, and a generous mouth. She wore a fashionable morning gown of jonquil silk and she looked both friendly and beautiful. Piers guessed she was his hostess, whom he had not laid eyes on in six years or so, but he was still relieved when Haggs removed doubt by introducing them.

"Irene, you remember my old friend Piers Withan? Now Lord Petteril, of course. Withy, my stepmother, Lady Haggard, in case you've forgotten!"

"How could I?" Piers said promptly, with a childish urge to cross his fingers behind his back. Instead, he took the lady's graciously proffered gloved hand and bowed over it while quickly searching her face for some distinguishing mark to remember her by. Perfectly arched black eyebrows, thicker and more dramatic than was fashionable, over unexpectedly light, hazel eyes.

"How do you do, Lady Haggard?" he said politely. "Thank you for inviting me at such short notice."

"It was more of a plea than an invitation," she replied, smiling up at him. "You look...different."

"He's merely a fashionable fribble nowadays," Haggs mocked, flicking at one of the two quizzing glasses hung around Piers's neck on black ribbons.

"I owe it to the title," Piers stated. "Next year, I'm going to cut my hair and buy pink pantaloons."

"Pink?" Lady Haggard said, her lips twitching.

"Pink," Piers said firmly. "Someone told me they were all the crack."

"He's lying," Haggs said. "Same old Withy as you see. Is that April skulking behind you?"

"I ain't skulking," April retorted.

"Ah," said Lady Haggard, looking her over with interest. "So you are the famous April? No one told me you were so pretty."

"I ain't," April muttered.

"Don't contradict the lady of the house," Piers said. He held Lady Haggard's gaze. "April is my assistant, as you know."

"I will make sure the servants understand," Lady Haggard said smoothly. "Come, let us go inside before you meet the others."

"What others?" Piers asked Haggs as they followed her across the gravel to the front steps, April trailing behind.

"Part of the problem," Haggs said ruefully. "Got a bit of a party staying here—including your aunt, the dowager, I'm afraid."

There was no reason for Haggs to blush while he spoke of Aunt Hortensia, the formidable Dowager Lady Petteril. Piers reached the obvious conclusion. "With my cousin Gussie? Who is my aunt trying to marry her to now? Not you?"

"Randall Hope, I suspect. He's Lord Gardham's heir. Decent match."

Over my dead body.

"Just before Peter shows you your room," Lady Haggard said, crossing a finely panelled entrance hall, "let me show you our accident."

She threw open a door on the left, and they all trailed after her into a light, bright room at the corner of the house. It had three windows on one side, and two on the other. A few portraits stood on the floor, leaning against the wall. An easel, covered with a large rough, paint-strewn cloth, drew all eyes to the centre of the room.

"I commissioned the portraitist, Claude St. Etienne, to paint Peter," Lady Haggard said.

"Is this it?" Piers asked, indicating the covered easel.

"No. He hasn't started on me yet," Haggs said. "Claims he needs to be better acquainted with me first. While he's becoming so, Irene persuaded him to clean up some of the ancestors. This," Haggs added, tugging off the cover, "is my father."

Sir Weston Haggard had been a distinguished man, his harsh features, so far as Piers recalled, similar to his son's, but without the humour or easy-going nature. Even so, there had been something about him that compelled respect and liking. The man in the portrait, an adoring hound at his feet, held his slightly grizzled head at an arrogant angle. For an instant, Piers thought the artist had painted him blindfolded for some reason, then realized it was merely a thick line of black paint slashed across the picture. It dripped down Sir Weston's cheeks and clothes, too, looking unpleasantly like dried blood.

Startled, Piers swung his gaze on Haggs and then his stepmother.

"Cor," April said. "You got kids staying here, mister? I mean sir."

"No," Haggs said, staring at her. "You think a *child* would do something like this?"

"Childish thing to do," April said. "Doesn't hurt him though, does it?"

Both Haggs and his stepmother gazed at her with a mixture of fascination and consternation.

"Nothing can hurt *him*," Piers agreed. "But the aim could well have been to pain his family. Where did this damage occur?"

"Right here," Lady Haggard said, gesturing to where the easel stood.

"St. Etienne was cleaning it," Haggs added.

Piers blinked. "Why? Surely it was only a few years old?"

"Eight," Lady Haggard said. "But it hung in the dining room where there was a bit of an accident when they were sweeping the chimney. Everything got covered in soot, including Weston's portrait."

"Unfortunate painting," Piers murmured. "Can it be repaired?"

"St. Etienne says so," Haggs replied, "though he seems to be taking the damage as a personal insult."

"Could it be?" Piers asked, lifting one of his quizzing glasses to more closely examine the picture. The slash of black was straight and bold as though made with one violent stroke of the brush, defacing both Sir Weston's face and a chunk of sky on either side.

Lady Haggard frowned, uncomprehending. "Could it be an insult to Monsieur St. Etienne? Well, he painted it in the first place. But who would damage our property merely to annoy an artist?"

"Another artist?" April suggested. Then she shrugged. "Does it matter? Since it can be fixed."

Haggs and his stepmother regarded her as though she had grown horns.

"There is an abuse of trust," Piers said. "Or friendship. Or at least hospitality. When did it happen?"

"During the night before last," Haggs said. "Tuesday. St. Etienne discovered it the following morning, and that's when I wrote to you to come and give us the benefit of your wisdom."

Piers met his gaze. "Who do you think did it?"

"If I knew that, I'd kick them out the house."

"Yes, but who do you *think*?" April said impatiently.

Lady Haggard blinked at her.

Haggs looked at Piers. "I honestly don't know. I cannot think the servants would either want or dare to do such a thing. Nor can I imagine our guests behaving so badly. And yet there it sits. Defaced."

"*Are* there other artists present?" Piers enquired.

Haggs shook his head.

"What about visiting servants?" April asked. "They might be resentful, either on their own account or their master's. Or mistress's."

"They'd lose their position for a moment of temper," Lady Haggard pointed out. "But this room was not locked. Anyone could have done it. I just cannot imagine who or why."

Piers scratched his chin.

Haggs threw the cover back over the defaced portrait. "Come. Now you've seen the worst, I'll show you to your room. Then you can meet our other guests."

HIS LORDSHIP WOULD hate meeting all the Haggards' guests at once. He had a problem with faces. April wondered if she could hover in the background, so that she could find out who they all were. Then she remembered she was angry with him, and glared instead at Lady Haggard who had also remained in the room when the two men went off together.

The lady didn't look haughty. On the other hand, she did seem amused which wasn't quite the reaction April had hoped for.

"So, April," Lady Haggard said. "What shall I do with you?"

"Nothing," April said breezily. "Expect I'll be gone in a couple of hours. To Sillitrees with Mr. Stewart."

Lady Haggard leaned toward her. "Who is Mr. Stewart?"

"His lordship's valet."

"I see. Sir Peter led me to believe you prefer to stay with his lordship."

"Depends if he needs me," April said, deliberately careless.

"You don't think he needs you here?"

"Nah. You won't want me under your feet neither."

Unexpectedly, Lady Haggard caught and held April's gaze. "Oh, I can keep you very busy and very safe. Is it me or Lord Petteril you are trying to avoid

"You," April replied with hostility. "No reason to avoid him, have I?"

"You have no reason to avoid me either. Yet. I won't tolerate rudeness in my own house, April, but certainly, you had better stay here until either of you decides otherwise."

Heat burned in April's cheeks. Her hostility had nothing to do with the woman bearing the brunt of it, which made her both ashamed and angry.

"Come with me," Lady Haggard said briskly. "Deal—my maid—will look after you. She'll be kind, too, unless you're rude."

As Lady Haggard swept toward the door, April remained frozen to the spot. "I work for Lord Petteril," she said. "That ain't going to change."

"Not unless he dismisses you," Lady Haggard said, "for disobedience."

Damn him! Damn her. But still she followed the lady from the room and upstairs to her boudoir.

Chapter Two

"She doesn't show it," Haggs said, sprawling in the chair by the fireside in Piers's bedchamber. "But this has really upset Irene."

Piers turned back from the window, which looked out over some neat parkland toward a wood. "Because the portrait is of your father? Or is it the malice behind such an act that appals her?"

Haggs shrugged. "Both, I should think. But you understand the awkwardness of the situation. Someone in the house must have done it, which is bad enough. But how does one find out without offending all one's honoured guests?"

"Well, who *could* have done it?"

"Anyone. The room was never locked."

"Was it used only by the painter himself? St. Etienne?"

Haggs nodded. "Ever since he arrived at the beginning of June. About a fortnight ago, now. He likes the light there and it's where I'm supposed to sit for him when he decides it's time. And anyone else who commissions him while he is in residence, I suppose."

"He is eager for commissions?" Piers asked. "His career is not thriving?"

"I suspect not, just at the moment. Which is no doubt why he is willing to undertake such a menial task as cleaning and repairing old pictures. But he painted the defaced portrait in the first place. Eight years ago, apparently, when I first went up to Oxford."

"Could he have done the damage himself to make more work?" Piers wondered.

"What a devious mind you have."

10

"Then he could have?"

Haggs shrugged. "He could have. Anyone could have."

"Even you? In theory."

"In theory, yes. In practice, while the old gentleman and I didn't precisely get along, I would hardly do something as mindlessly destructive as defacing his portrait two years after his death."

"I know," Piers said, still watching him. "Can you think of anyone who might? In a moment of rage?"

"Who would be that enraged after all this time? Is this your way of asking if my stepmother might have done it?"

Piers held his gaze. "Probably, it's my way of asking if you really want to know who did it. It may mean raking up a good deal of information you don't really want to know."

Haggs scowled. "Like all the damning things we discovered about the Bootles last month?"

"Well, that was a murder, with which they were about to charge a friend of ours," Piers said. "This is a far lesser crime, and stinks of spite rather than evil."

Haggs sprang up and paced across the room and back. He halted just in front of Piers. "We need to know. I don't want someone so spiteful in my house, pretending to be a friend or a loyal servant or whatever. I can understand your distaste—after all, your aunt and cousin are here too—so don't feel obliged to stay. I know you have much to do at Sillitrees."

"Don't be daft. Of course I shall help, if you're sure you want to know."

Haggs nodded curtly. "I'll leave you to wash and change if you want to. Come down to the garden when you're ready. We're having tea there. Oh." He paused, frowning, his hand on the door knob. "What is the matter with April? She seems grumpy rather than impudent."

Piers's smile was twisted. "She's afraid I brought her here to dump her on Lady Haggard."

"Did you?"

"No," Piers said. "I brought her because she's damned useful at solving puzzles."

TEN MINUTES LATER, washed and wearing the fresh morning clothes from his over-night bag, he remembered to check his appearance in the looking glass. In buff pantaloons and a well-cut blue coat, his snowy white cravat held in place by a plain gold pin, his quizzing glasses dangling from his neck, he supposed he looked smart enough. Apart from his rather wild chestnut locks which tended either to stick up or flop around his face. Trying to care, he dragged the brush through his hair once, then lost interest. He was the viscount. A certain haughtiness entered his eyes and stretched his distantly smiling lips.

In a crowd of new people, he would be lucky to pick out his host and hostess, let alone anyone else he had met before. Apart from Aunt Hortensia. He always seemed to recognize her. Probably because she could hardly bear to look at him.

He sauntered downstairs, where a servant directed him through another salon to the French doors and into the garden at the back of the house.

A sea of faces turned toward him.

"Piers!" yelped the joyful, and blessedly familiar voice of his little cousin Gussie. She even leapt to her feet before Aunt Hortensia yanked her back down again.

"Well," drawled a throaty voice close by. "Who, my dear is that?"

Piers did not spare her a glance. She was not addressing him. Fortunately, someone had already taken his arm—black eyebrows, jonquil dress and a charmingly light voice as she said, "Lord Petteril, allow me to present our other guests to you."

Of course, it was Lady Haggard. Since she seemed inclined to present him as some kind of trophy, he kept in place the haughty viscount, who would expect no less.

"Of course, there is no need to present your aunt or cousin," she said gaily, "but here are our good friends Mr. and Mrs. Laughton and Mrs. Bramley, Miss Marianne Orville, my niece, my nephew the Reverend Mr. Kenneth Orville. Here is Mr. Hope. And of course, the great portrait painter, Monsieur Claude St. Etienne. Everyone, this is a very good friend of Peter's—and therefore of mine—Lord Petteril."

Petteril bowed distantly to the company. There was little time to do more and in any case, he did not stand a chance of putting names to faces, apart from Monsieur St. Etienne, who sat alone.

He looked to be in his forties and was very thin, his eyes and mouth drooping with discontent and perhaps a hint of contempt. His reddish hair, streaked with grey on one side, was too long for fashion and a shade unkempt.

"Come and have a cup of tea," Lady Haggard said.

Since she still had hold of his arm, it was easy to give a faint tug in the direction of St. Etienne. She followed his lead as smoothly as if they had been waltzing. St. Etienne looked surprised but not particularly gratified. A footman appeared to hold her ladyship's chair, another to lay teacups and saucers and plates upon the table. A fresh tea pot was laid before Lady Haggard, and a plate of tiny sandwiches and savoury pastries set in the middle.

"What an honour to meet you, monsieur," Petteril said, his cool, aloof voice in stark contrast to the warm words. He always thought that a nice touch.

"You are kind," St. Etienne said dismissively.

"Rarely," Petteril murmured. "I am, however, shocked to see your portrait of the late Sir Weston so defaced. Thank you," he added to his hostess as he received his cup of tea.

"A crime most senseless and spiteful," St. Etienne snapped.

His eyes definitely flashed with outrage, and yet behind the anger was a trace of some other emotion Piers could not quite put his finger on.

"Certainly, it makes no sense to us," Piers agreed. "But there must be a reason in the perpetrator's mind. Were you happy with the portrait? Was it your best work?"

The artist frowned, staring at him. "No," he said. "An artist is never entirely happy with his work. And assuredly, I have done better. And worse. Sir Weston was a man of character. My painting showed at least some of that and I am not ashamed of it—if that is what you mean to imply? That I destroyed my own work in a fit of—what? Pique? Unworthiness? Frustration at my lack of talent?"

The Frenchman spoke English very well, only a hint of French accent remaining, though his voice was rough, a little too high and grating.

"I implied nothing," Piers said mildly. "But I thank you for the information."

"What information?" St. Etienne growled.

"Your assessment of the portrait, of course."

Lady Haggard leaned forward, offering the plate of sandwiches to each of them. "Lord Petteril is academically inclined and excellent with puzzles. Peter and I have asked him to help us discover who did this. I know you feel almost as strongly as we do about the incident. You will excuse me while I play hostess once more."

Piers rose at once, bowing as she flitted off. St. Etienne barely bumped his backside up and down on his chair. Piers resumed his seat.

"An academic viscount in pursuit of vandals," St. Etienne said with a curl of his lip. "How...unique."

"Indubitably," Piers agreed, popping a sandwich into his mouth. Keeping his gaze on the painter, he chewed, swallowed and reached for another. "So, tell me, when exactly did you last see Sir Weston's portrait *un*damaged?"

"The evening before last—Tuesday. Does that information teach you anything?"

"Not yet. Perhaps you could be more specific. What time on Tuesday evening?"

"After dinner. Instead of accompanying the gentlemen to the drawing room, I went to my studio—the room allotted me by Lady Haggard. It was perhaps half past nine."

"What did you do? Some cleaning of the portrait?"

"No. I made some sketches of Sir Peter. Her ladyship has commissioned a portrait of him."

"Did he sit for you?" Piers asked.

"No, I sketched from memory." With exaggerated patience, he added, "Watching Sir Peter during dinner, I had various ideas for poses, expressions, and I wanted to put them on paper, to see which, if any, might work."

"Was Sir Weston's portrait covered when you went into the room?"

"No. I glanced at it before I left, and it was not defaced."

"And what time was that?"

"I did not look."

"But you have some idea. Was the house quiet? Had everyone gone to bed? Were the servants still up?"

"It must have been after eleven," St. Etienne said impatiently. "Most of the guests had retired, but I could hear someone playing in the billiard room."

"I don't suppose you know who that was? Or even how many people were playing?"

St. Etienne shrugged. "Mr. Hope, probably. I am sure I heard him laugh as I went upstairs, but I do not know if he was alone or if anyone else was with him."

"Did you see anyone else? Guests? Servants? Family?"

The artist thought about it in an exaggerated sort of a way. "No," he said finally.

"And the next time you saw the portrait?"

"The following morning at nine of the clock when I entered the studio."

"Was the portrait covered?"

"No. The damage was obvious as soon as I walked in."

Piers sipped his tea and set the cup down in its saucer. "How wet was the paint?"

St. Etienne's eyes widened. "I did not touch it. But...it glistened. It was more than tacky."

"Can you guess from that when the damage was done?"

St. Etienne thought about it. "Not really." He sounded disappointed. "The paint was pretty thick. I would say a few hours, probably no more than eight, but that does not really help us."

"What did you do?" Piers asked him. "When you discovered the damage?"

"I shouted and servants came running, then Sir Peter and guests—"

"All the guests?"

"It seemed so, everyone crowded into the studio, staring at the destruction."

"Did they all look shocked? Surprised?"

"Of course!"

"No one whose reaction seemed wrong to you?"

St. Etienne stared at him, a frown tugging at his brows. But at least he seemed to be thinking about it. "Not that I noticed," he said reluctantly.

"But the destruction is not total, is it?" Piers said, helping himself to a small pastry. "Lady Haggard tells me you can repair it."

"Of course," St. Etienne said haughtily.

A young lady of only seventeen summers rushed up to them. "Piers, how wonderful to see you!"

Only Gussie ever greeted him with that particular kind of enthusiasm. Piers rose and kissed her smiling cheek. Inevitably, Aunt Hortensia was behind her. He bowed over her reluctant hand.

Aunt Hortensia, the Dowager Lady Petteril, sniffed. "Lady Haggard did not tell us you were expected."

"I imagine she didn't want you to bolt," Piers said. "What a very fetching gown, Gussie. Breaking hearts?"

"Oh, I do hope so," Gussie said, blushing and smiling at him.

"And you will not stand in her way," Aunt Hortensia stated, glaring at him.

"Only if it is Gussie's heart in question," Piers said amiably.

Aunt Hortensia sniffed again. "Come, Augusta." She paused, just as Piers was about to sit down again. "By the way, I have still heard nothing from Bertie."

"I'm sure that's a good thing," Piers said, and sat down at last, watching their backs retreat toward the house.

"Who is Bertie?" St. Etienne enquired.

"Another cousin. My aunt's favoured nephew who recently went to the Peninsula." In fact, he had transferred from the Guards to a fighting regiment, with a commission bought by Piers.

"She does not like you, Milady Petteril."

"With such skills of observation," Piers said, "you should be an artist."

Rather to his surprise, St. Etienne did not look remotely offended. In fact, he smiled. "Fortunately for you, I am. I like your face. I am prepared to paint you."

CLAUDE ST. ETIENNE watched Viscount Petteril walk away from him with faint stirrings of artistic excitement. Although he was bored painting dull portraits of wealthy English people, he could no longer afford to be choosy. For the last couple of years, gritting his teeth, he had desperately tried to revive his fortunes with likenesses of pompous aristocrats and their pampered wives. Searching avidly for some kind of rarity or contradiction in their character, he had frequently resorted to fantasy to add interest or glamour, mostly of the flattering variety.

This Petteril, however, he had no need to flatter and he had no difficulty in discovering contradictions and points of fascination in his face. He was a good looking young man, a mixture of scruffy hair and well cut, conventional clothes. A high, intelligent forehead, lazy, dark eyes that occasionally shot alarmingly perceptive bolts and missed little. A man who wore a mask of haughtiness and concealed low self-confidence not very far beneath his skin. St. Etienne had caught a glimpse of weary hurt in the viscount's veiled eyes when the old harridan had attacked him. The little Gussie was fond of him, though, and he was unexpectedly protective of her.

An *affaire du cœur*? St. Etienne doubted it. But it was during this brief encounter that he realized he had finally found a subject worth painting.

Peter Haggard was all very well—he liked the rough ugliness of his face, so similar to his father's. But he was too open to appeal to St. Etienne's art. Perhaps he could paint them side by side—if not on the same canvas, then on adjacent ones.

Maybe this viscount could even discover who defaced Sir Weston's portrait, though he doubted it. So many people disliked St. Etienne just because he was French and not even aristocratic by birth, that there were far too many suspects. The great Lord Petteril would chase his own tail, which might be even more amusing.

While Haggard would not grudge St. Etienne's extra fee for repairing the portrait.

When all the other guests had gone inside to while away the time before supper, St. Etienne followed them, and went straight to the room he had appropriated as his "studio".

Throwing himself down in the seat at the desk, he seized some paper and charcoal and began to sketch the viscount. So lost was he in the task, that it was some time before he realized he was not alone.

Whipping his head around, he saw a strange girl in a maid's mob cap and an old fashioned dress in a faded shade somewhere between lavender and a dusky pink. Unexpectedly, it had old, damaged lace stitched to the collar and sleeves, and she wore a large, leather purse at the belt around her waist. Strands of golden blonde hair had escaped the cap. Deep blue eyes stared at him with all the knowledge and wisdom of a very old woman, and yet her face was young, vital, even beautiful despite the slightly retrousse nose and a mouth that was too wide.

His artistic muse, already sparked by Lord Petteril, flamed now with more than a hint of desire. Under her steady gaze, he rose and came toward her, walking around her to let the late afternoon light play on the soft angles of her face, and glint among her escaped locks of golden hair.

"You, I will definitely paint," he announced.

"No you won't. I ain't got time for that stuff."

He blinked. "*Diable*. Who are you? You are not part of the household."

She moved nearer the easel with its defaced portrait, gazing at it with interest. "No. I'm April, Lord Petteril's assistant."

"Are you, by God?" asked another amused voice from the doorway.

Randal Hope, handsome and self-possessed, leaned against the door frame, twinkling eyes on Petteril's "assistant" with blatant admiration. "Well, I must say he's more daring than he used to be. Not sure it's very good taste, though, to inflict one's doxy on a lady's household."

"Don't suppose he ever has, then," April said with apparent indifference, though St. Etienne could see the spurt of fury in her thinned lips and the sudden rigidity of her stance. She turned away from the easel, marching toward Hope and the door. "'Scuse me."

But, of course, Hope was far too entitled to ever stand aside for a mere maidservant. St. Etienne felt a surge of helpless rage. He did not want to lose his lovely muse so soon, but he could do nothing against Hope, who despised the artist for his profession, his birth, and his race.

"What's your hurry, my rough little nymph?" Hope drawled with amusement. "Your master learned the value of sharing his toys a long time ago." Unhurriedly, he lifted his hand toward her neck.

At the same time, April's leg moved.

My God, she isn't, is she? Would she really knee him in the groin before he had even touched her? She would be dismissed without a character! In the hope of at least distracting one or both, St. Etienne charged across the room.

Hope did not so much as glance at him. St. Etienne cleared his throat to say something inane that might just get both him and the girl out of the room, even if it also got St. Etienne bullied out of the house.

And then, abruptly, they were saved.

A very large, fit young footman called William, loomed behind Hope. "Miss April? His lordship wants you immediately."

Chapter Three

As the unpleasant gent swung around on the footman, April straightened her threatening knee and returned her foot to the floor.

"Where is he?" she asked cheerfully and slid past the so-called gentleman while he was distracted. "Will you show me?"

"This way," the footman said briskly, and she hurried after him to the servants' stairs at the back of the house. Here, he glared at her. "What you thinking of, being in there? Especially with both of them!"

"I went to look again at the damage to the portrait," she replied. "Then *he* comes in and doesn't even notice me. Is he the artist?"

"Mr. St. Etienne is, yes," the footman said bitterly. "He's bad enough but that Mr. Hope is a menace. The maids aren't allowed to go into Hope's room for their own safety. Never be alone with him."

"Thanks for the warning," April said with a shiver. "And for the rescue. Sorry, I've forgotten your name?"

"William. I'm the third footman at Pelton Park."

"April. Lord Petteril's assistant."

"Seriously? What do you assist him with?"

"Whatever he needs. Decorating, cleaning, taking notes. It ain't true what that Hope cove said. His lordship wouldn't take advantage of anyone."

"Her ladyship's not a fool neither. Miss Deal, her maid, says we're to be polite to you."

"Well, as long as you are, I'll be polite to you, too."

William regarded her, half resentful, half amused. April grinned at him and heard his breath catch.

Hastily, he pushed open the landing door. "He's over there, in the library."

"Of course he is," April said happily. "Thanks, William!"

Forgetting she was angry with Lord Petteril, she all but skipped across the passage, remembered to knock, and then entered the library.

His lordship sat alone in one of the comfortable chairs by the empty fireplace. In deep thought, his long legs stretched out in front of him, his hands behind his head, he looked extraordinarily comfortable and relaxed. In fact, he didn't even notice she had come in until she stood right in front of him, her hands clasped behind her back.

He blinked and refocused on her. A spontaneous smile lit his dark eyes. "April. Is it bearable for a day or so?"

He didn't sound as if he planned to leave her behind, so she answered truthfully, "Deal's not so bad, though she looks at me as if I'm one of your old books in Greek. Lady Haggs is kind but she don't want me disrupting the house, which I suppose is fair enough. Went to talk to the artist but didn't get much chance. Don't like that Hope cove, though. Good thing if it were him wrecked the painting 'cause he's a menace to females. Needs a good kick in the—"

His lordship sat up. "Yes, well, last resort, April. He's a vindictive bas—er...cove."

"You know him?"

"Used to. We were at school together. What did he do?"

"Nothing, just throwing his might around. The artist cove don't like him. I think he was going to intervene when William appeared and said you wanted me. William's a footman and he's huge and brawny."

"I know. I sent him to find you."

"He could be a friend. D'you think Hope done it?"

"Don't know yet. He was still up and in the right place after St. Etienne retired, apparently playing billiards just two doors along, probably between eleven and midnight and probably with at least one other person since St. Etienne heard him laugh."

April had her notebook out, scribbling down the times.

"And by nine the following morning, the portrait was damaged. But St. Etienne hadn't covered it, so any of the servants going in early in the morning could have seen it— or even done it—earlier than that."

April dropped her notebook back into the leather bag at her waist, then pulled up a footstool and sat at Lord Petteril's feet. It felt almost like home. Elbows on her knees, she rested her head in her hands and frowned with concentration.

"Who was the vandal getting at? The Haggards or the artist? Someone bear a grudge against the old gent?"

"Sir Weston's been dead for a little over two years," Petteril pointed out. "That slash of paint looks too angry, too spiteful to be an old grudge against him. If you didn't like the man, it's easy enough to politely decline his widow's invitation and keep your dignity." He shifted restlessly. "I'll have to speak to them all. Can you get details from the servants? Who went to bed when? Who went into the room first that morning? Who's responsible for cleaning it?"

"Servants would have to be crazy to destroy their master's property," April said, scowling at him. "They'd be bounced without a character, likely end up a canary bird into the bargain."

He understood she meant *imprisoned*, but said, "Does it seem the act of a particularly sane person to you?"

She closed her mouth. "No. Do you really think it was one of the servants?"

"We don't yet know that it was not."

After a few more moments of thought, the rumbling of carriage wheels disturbed April. She rose and went to the window. A familiar carriage was being driven slowly toward the stable by a familiar coachman.

"That's Mr. Stewart and the baggage. Will you keep him with you?"

He shifted restlessly. "Do you still want to go on to Sillitrees?"

"Nah, better help you out here," April said breezily. "I'll go see the horses, then skulk in the kitchen."

AFTER APRIL HAD LEFT the library, Piers rubbed his slightly stubbly chin in a rueful kind of way. While he was glad she appeared to have overcome her fear of abandonment, he could not help feeling that he was only putting off the inevitable, evil hour.

He had made mistake after mistake with her, and they were all bound to come home to roost soon enough.

In a weak moment, he had given her work in his stables, in her not very convincing guise as a boy, though he had quickly decided this would not do and that she would be safer in the house, as the girl she truly was.

The trouble—one of the many troubles—was that she was not cut out for indoor domestic service. So in another moment of madness, he had raised her to be his "assistant". She was bright, clever, and could now read and write with ever increasing skill. Whatever else, she was useful to him, but though he could control the behaviour of his own household, her place was undeniably ambivalent to most people. A female "assistant" fluent in thieves' cant with the accents of the gutter was not welcome in most houses.

He could do more to civilize her, of course. She learned quickly and she was an excellent mimic. But that would hardly solve the basic issue of her reputation. And besides, he didn't really want to change her. He liked her as she was.

Brooding, he rose and made his way to his own room to wait for Stewart.

Piers had never wanted a valet. He only tolerated Stewart because the man hardly spoke and had the knack of keeping his things tidy without treating him like a baby who could not dress himself. Besides,

Piers had felt the frequent presence of a manservant might prevent him falling too far into melancholia again, if only from sheer pride.

If Stewart ever suspected he was a safety net, he gave no sign of it.

"Good afternoon, my lord," he said civilly when Piers walked into the room. He was ferrying a pile of shirts to the wardrobe where Piers's coats and waistcoats already hung. "Would you like me to stay when I have unpacked, or press on to Sillitrees?"

"They're a bit pressed for space here. You'd have to share quarters."

"Then perhaps we should go on to Sillitrees, if Sir Peter can spare us fresh horses."

Piers turned away. Less than a month ago, Stewart had come roaring to his rescue in the fight to arrest a vicious criminal. Piers had been touched. And appalled by the fact that Sewart had also witnessed April's wild grief when she had thought Piers was dead.

"I shouldn't be long," Piers said. "And it would be good to have my quarters comfortable by the time I get there."

"Of course, sir. Do you want this coat cleaned before I go, or shall I take it with me?"

"Take it, since you've brought plenty of others." He moved toward the slightly scratched old desk. "I'd better write you a letter of authority in case the servants my uncle left there are difficult. Send me word if the problems are too great."

"Certainly, my lord."

"Make sure you get some tea in the kitchen before you go. It should only be another couple of hours to Sillitrees, so you'll be there before dark."

Stewart's departure left him vaguely dissatisfied with himself. Perhaps he should go and pick Gussie's brains and see what else he could learn about the damaged portrait. Though he wasn't sure he could face a round with Aunt Hortensia just yet.

Sighing, he set about changing for dinner. He wore a tasteful gold and diamond tie pin and engraved gold sleeve buttons. Then, remem-

bering first to brush his hair into some semblance of order, he went
downstairs to occupy the drawing room and wait for company.

Although he was early, he was not the first to arrive. His cousin
Gussie, all chestnut ringlets and vital prettiness, swung around from the
window. She smiled at once, although it struck him he had somehow
disappointed her. It wasn't difficult to guess how.

"Piers! You are early, too."

"Avoiding your mama?"

"As if I would," she said righteously. "Who are you avoiding?"

"No one. I was looking for company."

Her eyes widened. "Whose?"

"I was about to ask you the same question."

She blushed. "I asked you first."

"Then yours, of course. What do you know about this wretched
painting that was defaced?"

"Nothing," said Gussie, frowning. "It didn't seem worthy of much
notice before it was defaced. Although Sir Weston did look quite like
Sir Peter."

"Did you see it in St. Etienne's studio?"

"No, in the dining room. Oh, well yes, I saw it *once* in the studio. I
went for a peek after dinner on Tuesday."

"After the gentlemen had rejoined you in the drawing room?"

"Before." Her cheeks were quite pink.

"Assignation, Gussie?" he asked mildly.

"Not really. Or only for a moment."

"Dare I ask who with?"

"Such a nosy fellow," drawled another voice entirely. To Piers, it
sounded vaguely familiar, though he could not place it. He certainly
could not place the handsome, mocking face as the newcomer sauntered into the room. He had fashionably cut, short, fair hair and
seemed to favour the Corinthian look. "I had forgotten that."

Gussie seized Piers's hand, all but dragging him across the room. She was scarlet now, yet very pleased with herself at the same time.

"Oh, Piers, do you know Mr. Randal Hope? Sir, my cousin, Lord Petteril."

Well, that explained the familiar voice.

Casually Piers offered his hand. "How do you do? Must be ten years since we last met."

Hope touched his hand with a mere two fingers. "Indeed. And how elevated you have become. Somehow I never associated you with the Petteril title."

"Neither did I." It had taken the deaths of his uncle, his father, his brother and two cousins, all tragically close together.

But Hope's attention had already moved on, all his focus on Gussie. "Miss Withan, more enchanting than ever." There was no need to take her hand since they had met only a couple of hours ago, but he did so anyway, and made a meal of it. Piers suspected he would have kissed her fingers had she not hastily drawn them free—and she only did that, he was sure, because of Piers's presence. Why the devil were scoundrels and loose screws so attractive to her?

Piers watched Hope smile directly into Gussie's eyes, saw her dimple and flutter her eyelashes. *Oh, Gussie, Gussie.*

"So what brings your lordship to Pelton Park?" Hope said, refocusing on Piers once more.

"Sir Peter is one of his closest friends," Gussie answered for him. "Didn't you know?"

"Why no, I did not. I am closer to Lady Haggard than to her stepson." He caught Piers's eye and smiled. "That surprises you?"

"Only partially," Piers said ambiguously.

"Then what does bring you here? Lady Haggard did not appear to be expecting anyone else this week."

"It was a sudden invitation." On impulse, he added. "She asked for my help discovering who defaced her portrait of the late Sir Weston."

Hope laughed. "Oh, the poor lady! And you could not discover your way out of a paper parcel!"

"I confess I have never tried," Piers said. "Though I do recall discovering the way for many of us into the masters' good books at Harrow."

Hope curled his lips. "I am surprised you choose to remember that."

"I'm more surprised you do." Piers did not trouble to keep the amused contempt out of his voice this time, and Hope's eyes widened in amazement.

Gussie, glancing from one to the other in incomprehension, said, "What are you talking about?"

"Schoolboy errors," Piers said. "But Hope and I are quite used to helping each other out, are we not? So, tell me when you last saw Sir Weston's portrait undamaged."

"Not sure I ever did?"

"Not even when you sneaked in here to meet Gussie on Tuesday evening?"

Hope's eyes narrowed.

"I lit the lamps before you came," Gussie reminded him. "We remarked the likeness of the portrait to Sir Peter, don't you recall?"

"Perfectly," Hope said with a yawn. "But the artist fellow definitely saw it after us. He was in here long after we joined the ladies in the drawing room. He'd probably be more comfortable eating with the servants anyway. More his class of people."

"What a horrid old snob you are, sir," Gussie said with apparent affection, causing a faint flaring of Hope's nostrils.

"One thing about Gussie," Piers remarked. "She will always call a spade a spade. Did you see the portrait again, Hope? In its unaltered state."

"No," came the indifferent reply.

"Then how do you know St. Etienne was in the studio after you were?"

Hope stared at him. "Because when I went to play billiards, the lights were back on in there and I could hear him muttering to himself."

"Who did you play billiards with?"

"Laughton," Hope said curtly.

"Until when?"

"Damn it, how should I know? Midnight?"

"Were the lights still burning in the studio?" Piers asked.

"No idea. I didn't look. You've turned into a schoolmaster discovering who put the frog in his desk."

"They always knew exactly who put the frogs in their desks. Do you think Lady Haggard regards this crime in the same lighthearted manner?"

"If she does not, she should check out that other frog, St. Etienne. If you ask me, he's just drumming up business. Be a good fellow and go and bore someone else, hmm?"

He strolled away and, encountering Yates the butler with a tray of sherry, swiped a glass on the way past.

"Rude," Gussie observed.

Piers glanced at her to see if she meant him or Hope, but Lady Haggard came in just then with another lady and Piers tried desperately to recall who the devil she was. Why did women keep changing their gowns? He could never keep track of them by colour this way.

Since he ranked highest among the guests, he had the pleasure of escorting Lady Haggard into dinner. Haggs, poor soul, had less luck, with Aunt Hortensia on his arm.

"I must say I am thrilled to meet you at last," said the attractive lady on Piers's other side. He recognized her voice, a little husky and yet as smooth as warm, melted butter. "I have heard so much about you."

"The pleasure is all mine," Piers said gallantly. "Though I cannot think why you would have heard of me at all."

"My dear man, for at least two weeks after each of your visits to town, the ton speaks of no one else. Perhaps it is your erratic appearances and disappearances, while everyone else endures the entire Season. Mystery is irresistible to a lady, you know."

"Funnily enough, it is irresistible to me also."

Only a little later, he was encouraged to hear St. Etienne on her other side, address her as "Mrs. Laughton." Small, slightly pudgy fingers, pretty face, thick blonde hair and that so seductive voice.

"I was sorry to hear about this sad business with Sir Weston's portrait," he said to her when her somewhat silted conversation with St. Etienne paused for a moment. "Who on earth would do such a thing?"

Mrs. Laughton shuddered. "I cannot imagine. Such wanton destruction and so disrespectful to both the family and Monsieur St. Etienne."

Piers lowered his voice confidentially. "Then you do not hold with the views of some that St. Etienne is to blame for being French?"

"That is ridiculous. He cannot help where he was born and we have been harbouring French émigrés in this country for twenty years. On top of which he has more cause to hate Bonaparte and the revolutionaries than we have. He was driven from his home by them and forced to live in exile with a nation of philistines."

Somewhat startled by such vehemence, he raised his eyebrows. "Are we so very uncultured, ma'am?"

"Very," she said firmly, and then smiled. "Some of us. Do you care for art, my lord?"

"I do. Though I confess I care for people more. To deface a painting is a sin, but to upset Sir Weston's widow and son is unforgivable."

Mrs. Laughton's eyes fell. "You are right, of course. Dear Irene hides so much behind a smile."

"And she is determined to find the culprit. Did you see the portrait at all while it was in St. Etienne's studio?"

She hesitated, though he could not tell whether she was trying to remember or to decide whether or not to tell the truth.

"Yes," she said at last. "Twice, I think. Once when I wandered in to speak to Monsieur St. Etienne about a possible commission. And, of course, yesterday when we discovered the damage. Such a shock!"

"When was it you went to speak to Monsieur St. Etienne?"

"Tuesday afternoon." Her eyes held something of a challenge. "Why?"

"I am trying to discover exactly when the damage was done," he said. "In that way, we may be able to tell the culprit. Might I ask you—when did you retire on Tuesday night?"

"About eleven, when everyone else did."

"Not everyone. Monsieur St. Etienne remained in his studio after that. And I believe your husband and Mr. Hope played billiards until midnight."

"I am not surprised to hear it. Nor to realize that you already know more than I could tell you."

"Then you did not hear or see anything unusual during the night?"

Long, dark eyelashes fluttered, exotically long and dark in contrast with her fair hair and skin. He wondered if she darkened them.

"Nothing" she replied. "I sleep quite heavily in the country."

"So do I," Piers said, not entirely truthfully. "Quiet and fresh air, I suppose."

"Quiet?" Lady Haggard exclaimed on his other side. "In the midst of all the bird and animal racket from first light?"

"You do not sleep well in the country?" Piers asked.

Her eyes flickered. "Well enough," she drawled.

For the first time, he sensed deceit in her. Of course, people deceived each other all the time in trivial ways for myriad reasons. He was guilty of it himself. Still, the moment bothered him because it was such a silly thing to lie about. Now that he looked at her more closely, there were shadows of tiredness beneath her eyes, a certain brittle excitement in her quick laughter.

A suspicion hit him which probably had nothing to do with the defacing of the portrait, and yet it made him look at the whole matter differently.

Chapter Four

When the ladies had withdrawn and the port and brandy had been placed on the table, the atmosphere grew quickly more relaxed and much less formal.

Piers, nodding to the empty place on the wall above the fireplace, said to Haggs, "Is that where your father's portrait hung?"

Haggs nodded, pouring himself a glass of brandy and pushing the decanter toward the young, clerical gentleman, his cousin, Mr. Kenneth Orville. "Yes. Looks a bit empty, doesn't it?"

"At least you can't see the shape where it used to be," Orville said kindly.

"No, we had the room redecorated after the chimney disaster," Haggs said. "We swapped the other sooty pictures, but Irene was especially keen to keep my father's in its place." He raised his glass toward St. Etienne. "You really have your work cut out now."

St. Etienne grunted, taking a small paper packet from his pocket. He unfolded the paper, poured the powdered contents into his port and swirled the glass.

"For the migraine," he told Piers when he discovered him watching. "As for Sir Weston, I can take the black paint off easily enough. He will resume his place shortly."

Haggs nodded curtly, as he did when he was about to speak of something else entirely. But Piers did not want the subject changed.

"I think I only met Sir Weston once," he said. "A man of few words but great principles, I thought."

Haggs sipped his brandy. "A fair summation as usual."

"Hardly," Piers said. "There must have been more to him."

Haggs scowled at him, then smiled reluctantly. "Of course. Actually, he could be very charming when he chose to be, and funny. And though he was strict, he was never unkind."

"Sir Weston's family—indeed his whole household—were devoted to him," Kenneth Orville said. "Including me."

Haggs raised his glass in another silent toast to his cousin, but Piers only noticed it from the corner of his eye. He was watching the expressions of everyone else.

Hope looked sceptical in a bored kind of a way. Laughton's smile was twisted, almost bitter, though he smoothed it out very quickly. St. Etienne merely nodded, gazing into his glass before taking another sizeable swallow.

"Did you all know him well?" Piers asked.

Among the various sage and serious nods, Hope regarded Piers with open mockery. "More of your *discoveries*, my lord? Sounds a bit like nosiness to me. Sniffing out salacious gossip will hardly find you the culprit who damaged the portrait."

"What salacious gossip?" Piers enquired. "I never heard any."

"Well, you wouldn't, would you?" Hope retorted. "You hardly moved in the first circles until very recently."

"I assure you there never was any," Orville said, glaring at Hope. "My uncle was a good man. A great man, even."

"A man may be charming," Laughton observed, with a contemptuous glance at Hope, "without betraying his wife and family."

"My father never betrayed anyone," Haggs snapped.

"Of course he did not," Orville said indignantly. "Despite temptation dangled before him."

Laughton turned on Orville, his expression suddenly ugly, which was even more interesting.

"There is no scandal in that," Haggs snapped and glared at Piers. "After my mother died, my father was somewhat overwhelmed with young ladies eager to be Lady Haggard. I only wished I inherited half his allure."

"Don't rub it in, old fellow," Hope drawled. "The world already knows—all the world except his lordship—that Laughton was his wife's second choice. Sir Weston chose the divine Irene and the beauteous Susan, poor thing, had to resort to Laughton here."

Inevitably, Laughton sprang to his feet in fury, fists clenched as he glared down at the insolently smiling Hope.

"Oh, don't rise to him," Haggs said impatiently. "It's just his penchant for drama."

"Besides," Piers added. "His interpretations were always faulty."

Hope frowned in his direction. "What the devil do you mean by that?"

"Interpret it," Piers said gently, "as best you can."

"Perhaps we should join the ladies," Orville said.

"I second the proposal," Hope said. "After all, the best thing I know of his lordship is his exquisite cousin."

Piers sipped his brandy in a thoughtful kind of way. "Not sure I'd call Bertie exquisite."

It won him a laugh from all but Hope. Haggs asked if he had heard from Bertie since the new major had taken ship for Lisbon. Laughton sat down, and the conversation moved into safer channels. Inevitably, last month's shocking assassination of the prime minister was rehashed and reviled. Good things were expected of his successor, Lord Liverpool. The prospect of war with the United States was also touched upon, along with the progress of the eternal war with France, particularly on the peninsula. No one seemed to hold any objectionable views. And no one asked St. Etienne his opinion. Nor did he offer it.

"You were winding Hope up," Haggs murmured to Piers as they eventually led the others toward the drawing room. "Why? Think he did it?"

"Nah," Piers said in excellent imitation of April. "Don't like the cove."

AFTER SEVERAL INTERESTING discussions with the servants, whom she helped with clearing up after dinner, April went in search of his lordship. She had a nasty moment when she opened the library door and glimpsed the unspeakable Hope playing chess with Mr. Orville. Since there was no sign of Petteril, she hastily closed the door again before they noticed her.

She couldn't really go to his bedchamber to talk to him. Lady Haggs would throw her out, and all hell would break loose. Just thinking about it made her palms sweat. Instead, she went back down to the salon used as the artist's studio.

The lamps were lit only on one side. By their glow, Lord Petteril stood at the easel, staring at the damaged portrait.

"There you are," she muttered, hurrying in. "Went looking for you in the library but that Hope was there, playing chess with the vicar."

"Hope and Orville...curious pairing," Petteril said distractedly.

"What you doing?" April asked, glancing from the painting to his focused face.

He didn't answer directly but said. "It's splashed across his eyes like a blindfold."

"Does it matter where the paint went?"

"I think it might. Why the eyes? Why *his* eyes?"

"Makes no difference. Painting can't see, so no point in blocking its eyes."

"Except symbolically. For a man who has been dead two years, he still inspires powerful emotion."

"How d'you mean?"

"For one thing, he was popular with women."

April wrinkled her nose. "Oh. Another Hope who couldn't keep it in his breeches?"

"On the contrary, he seems to have been quite the virtuous husband. Which probably wasn't difficult since he was married to Irene. But apparently before he married her, several other women had set their caps at him. Including Mrs. Laughton. Laughton clearly feels he is second fiddle. Which Hope rubs in."

"But Mrs. Laughton is Lady Haggard's best friend," April said. "Or at least one of 'em. The other is that Mrs. Bramley, the widow. Do you suppose she was after the old gent too? And Lady Haggs immediately makes friends with her old rivals."

"Keeping her friends close and her enemies closer," Piers murmured. "I think I need to have another chat with her ladyship." His eyes focused on April properly. "What did you find out?"

"Bits and pieces. Cherry, the maid responsible for cleaning the ground floor rooms, told everyone she didn't clean the studio at all yesterday morning. But I finally got her to admit she went in there as early as five o'clock, to get ahead of her work before her half day. She saw the damaged portrait and bolted in case she got the blame."

"Understandable, if not very helpful. But at least that narrows down the timing of the damage by a few hours. I don't suppose the servants saw anyone creeping around between midnight and five in the morning?"

"Not that they're admitting to me. Yet. They're all very careful of their own masters and mistresses." April peered at the portrait. "So what's he not meant to see then with his eyes painted out?"

"Something or someone he would not have liked."

"Was Lady Haggs a good wife to him?"

"Haggs always thought so. He likes her, so does his sister. Haggs said she made his father happy again. Certainly he never regarded her in the evil stepmother mould. Apparently she was very cut up when Sir Weston died."

"But there are no other children. Maybe she didn't like him in her bed because he was old."

Lord Petteril blinked at her. "Maybe," he said doubtfully. "Doesn't match with his famous charm, though."

"Fantasy and reality ain't always the same."

"You're a cynical little creature for one so young."

"Old in sin, me. Or at least in looking at it."

But his lordship's attention had returned to the painting. "Lady Haggard was his wife. Haggs is his son. Surely it would be their sins he would not want to see."

"Don't know about her," April said, "but *he's* better'n most gentlemen. By far."

"He is," Petteril agreed. "The other family members are Kenneth and Marianne Orville, the children of Sir Weston's sister. But she seems even younger than Gussie and he's a clergyman, sincerely devoted to his uncle's memory. I can't imagine either of them doing anything very shameful."

"Can't tell by looks," April said darkly. "I know some nasty priests. Although, to be fair, they may not be real priests at all."

"I think we may take it Orville is a real priest. Sir Weston gave him the living he holds just a couple of hours from here."

"Makes him beholden," April said grudgingly.

Petteril changed the subject. "Hear any gossip about my little cousin Gussie?"

"Nah, I'd tell you right away. Why?"

"I think she might be playing with fire." He sighed. "Again."

"Probably her ma," April said. "Again."

He gave her a distracted half-smile. "I wouldn't be surprised. You had better go to bed if you're to be up early for more investigating."

"So had you."

"Indeed. Use the servants' stairs."

"Don't I always?" she said indignantly.

"No."

She grinned and left him. Though she *did* take the servants' stairs up to the attic room she shared with Miss Deal. She was in no hurry to encounter the unspeakable Hope again, anywhere.

DELIBERATELY STOPPING himself from going after her to make sure she went straight to the green baize door to the servants' quarters, Piers forced his attention back to the damaged painting. He began to look around for St. Etienne's paints. He found a wooden travelling chest on the nearest table to the easel. Inside it were various pots and jars of paints made up and also the dry pigment ingredients in phials. The brushes, in a drawer at the bottom of the chest, were spotlessly clean.

Piers made a mental note to ask St. Etienne if he had left paint and brushes out, though even put away they would have been easy enough for the vandal to find. He also wanted to know if St. Etienne had cleared up, or if the vandal had.

He closed the chest and wandered out, deep in thought. Pausing on the first floor landing, he thought of going to the library to see if Hope and Orville were still there. He should probably make some kind of peace with Hope. Winding him up had been irresistible—Piers had been unreasonably annoyed to find the man unchanged from school days. Even those who did improve often did not think of their childhood behaviour—Piers's brother and his cousin John to name but two. But Hope irritated him because he quite clearly did remember, even dwelled on it and saw nothing wrong in what he had done or didn't do.

Which meant he was still a vindictive sod and quite capable of taking his revenge via April or Gussie. First thing tomorrow, he must speak to his little cousin.

Turning right at the next landing, he walked on toward his bedchamber. He knew he was the only non-family male to be quartered on this side of the house, so he was not particularly surprised to see a lady walking along the passage toward him.

She inclined her head. "Lord Petteril."

No butter voice or blonde hair, so not Mrs. Laughton. No dramatically black hair and brows like Irene Haggard, and she was certainly not his aunt or little cousin or the youthful Marianne Orville. Which left only one possibility—the widowed friend.

He bowed. "Mrs. Bramley."

Her hair was an unremarkable shade of brown, but it shone with health. Her face, pleasing rather than beautiful, held more intelligence than charm. In the dim lamplight of the passage, her vital blue eyes gave little clue as to her character. It was her mouth that kept Pier's attention—soft and generous, it lent a hint of vulnerability to her capable countenance, and also hinted at humour. A subtle lady, Mrs. Bramley, but an unexpectedly intriguing one. Especially as she paused beside him rather than hurrying on her way.

"We have only been introduced at a distance," she said lightly. "But you should know I am a great friend of Irene Haggard's."

"I am very glad to hear it," he said politely.

"I thought you might be interested in the fact," Mrs. Bramley said, holding his gaze. "Since Irene just told me about your discussion in the dining room after dinner."

"Lady Haggard was not there," he pointed out.

"Then you deny asking questions about Sir Weston and how he was regarded?"

"No."

She smiled suddenly, and he noticed the rather charming little laughter lines that formed around the corners of her eyes. "You need not hide that you are seeking the vandal for Irene and Peter. She told me that, too. So you might like to know that I also—er...set my cap at Sir Weston after he was widowed. Irene and I were already friends and I did not grudge her winning the prize. At least, not very much."

"Thank you," he said genuinely. "That cannot have been easy to say to a stranger."

"Not as hard as it might have been. You have a kind face, my lord."

He was not quite sure what to say to that so he merely asked if he might speak to her a little further in the morning.

"Of course," she said. "I ride early each day at first light. Good night, my lord."

So did he, as a rule. "Good night, Mrs. Bramley."

He was not really thinking of damaged portraits as he let himself in to his bedchamber. Life always held more possibilities...

WHEN THE NEXT KNOCK sounded at her door, Irene, Lady Haggard, closed her eyes with brief but heartfelt gratitude.

Rising from the chair before her dressing table, she tightened the ties of her lace and silk robe, hurried to the door, and opened it as softly as she could.

Claude St. Etienne, in shirt sleeves and without his cravat, slipped inside and silently closed the door before turning the key in the lock.

"I was afraid you would not come," Irene said unsteadily. "After the last two nights..."

"I was plagued by a migraine then. Tonight, it is better."

"I thought you might give up. Jane Bramley was with me for nearly an hour."

"I know. And then I had to wait another five minutes while she accosted the nosy milord."

"Lord Petteril is not nosy," Irene said, slipping into St. Etienne's arms. "We have asked him to find out who damaged the portrait. Peter says he is very good at such things."

"Well, remember you may not like the result."

"I can't imagine I ever would like it. What do you suppose Jane wanted with him? I suppose he is dreadfully attractive, even if he is only the same age as Peter. There is something about his eyes when he deigns to give one all his attention. All that focus... Oh, hold me, Claude."

He obliged, kissing her hungrily and moving her by slow, teasing increments toward the bed. But his hands were already inside her robe, and the sweetness of satisfaction was almost upon her.

Oh yes, everything would be fine now. Everything would be wonderful.

Chapter Five

The following morning, April hurried down the servants' stairs from her shared attic bedroom, looking forward to a brisk walk in the fresh air. She would rather have practiced her riding, now that they were in the country again, but servants did not ride for pleasure, and besides, his lordship had sent all the horses bar the greys to Sil-litrees.

The door from the second floor hall burst open so suddenly she was almost sent flying, first by the swinging door and then by the liveried footman who charged through it so furiously, carrying a large, heavy tray.

"What's the matter with you?" April demanded.

It was William, who had rescued her from the unspeakable Hope. He pulled up in astonishment, irritation turning to shame. "Oh God, did I hit you with that door?"

"No and you didn't quite run over me neither but only because I'm used to dodging." April continued down the stairs in front of him, speaking over her shoulder. "What's put you in such a temper?"

William was still scowling. "Damn frog demands tea at this unholy hour and then he isn't even there to drink it! So I got to take it all the way back down again."

"Mr. St. Etienne? You could just have left it for him. If he's gone for a walk or a ride, he'll likely want it when he comes back."

"It will be cold and he'll want more."

"Well, he's probably in his studio already."

"Then he's been there all night, for his bed isn't slept in!" William bit his lip, clearly knowing he'd said too much.

At the door to the ground floor hall, as if still fighting the unreasonable desire to thwart the Frenchman any way he could, he hesitated.

"Wait one second," April commanded. "I'll just nip over and see."

Since the hall was empty save for Cheryl the maid scrubbing the doorstep, April sprinted across to the studio and found it totally empty. The damaged portrait stood on its easel exactly where it had been last night. The whole room looked as it had when she left Lord Petteril there the evening before.

She hurried back to William, who waited for her, still holding his tray, brows raised. She shook her head and his lip curled with as much distaste as anger.

"What's it to you?" April asked curiously. "It's not our business where they go."

"Time the bastard *did* go," William muttered. He glared at her. "Sorry for swearing. Where you off to, anyway?"

"Just a quick walk. His lordship always rides early, so he won't need me before breakfast." She cast him a wave, turning toward the narrow passage to the back door.

"Wait," William said, suddenly angry again. "What did you mean when you said you're used to dodging? Dodging blows? Does he hit you?"

April turned back, uncomprehending for the first instant. "He?" Her eyes widened. "Lord Petteril? Don't be stupid! Wouldn't be here if he did."

Annoyed on Petteril's behalf, she flounced out the door. Only as she strode around the building toward the stables did she wonder if it was true—*would* she stay if Petteril hit her? She had hung around other people, like Lord the thief and customers at the Silver Jug alehouse who had aimed so many blows at her that some had inevitably connected.

She wouldn't go near such people now, of course. Petteril had shown her that violence didn't have to be a way of life, that it wasn't necessary to earn respect. In fact, even while she'd been dodging the kicks and back handers, and grasping eagerly at whatever food or coins were flung her way, she hadn't respected any of those ham-fisted clunches. She hadn't known what respect meant.

She respected Lord Petteril, though. She'd do anything for him, and in her heart, she knew that he would never hit anyone who couldn't hit back.

April *always* hit back. She'd have kneed the unspeakable Hope where it hurt most. But Petteril never struck his servants. He never threw things at them or even shouted at them. And yet April never ever wanted him to be angry with her.

If he was angry, if he did *hit me, would I stay?*

It boggled her mind somewhat. Eventually, she decided she would just hit him back and wait for him to calm down. Then, turning into the stable yard, she suddenly saw him, in his most casual riding dress, leading out one of Sir Peter's horses and for no reason, her insides jolted. Her whole internal argument about what to do if he ever struck her dissolved into nothing.

It would never happen.

It came to her with another lurch that she trusted him, not just in that but in everything. She'd never trusted anyone before and just for a moment, it terrified her.

He came toward her, frowning, and she almost bolted.

"What is it?" he asked.

"Nothing," she said aggressively. Then, flushing, "That is, St. Etienne didn't sleep in his own bed last night and he's not in his studio."

His brows twitched. "Ah." His eyes searched hers. "I don't suppose you know whose bed he did sleep in?"

She drew in her breath. "William was so angry, I think it must be Lady Haggard's."

"No wonder she looks tired. So the servants know?"

"I suppose her own do, but they won't gossip to outsiders."

"William did."

"He was angry and he didn't say it was her in so many words." More reluctantly, she said, "He doesn't like the French."

"He's not the only one."

"Do you suppose that was the point of blocking out Sir Weston's eyes on the painting?" she blurted. "To stop him seeing what his widow was up to?"

"Or at least making the point."

"She might have done it herself in a moment of shame," April pointed out.

"Not sure she has anything to be ashamed of. Her husband's dead and she's betraying no one. Why shouldn't she seize a little happiness?"

"Would Sir Peter see it that way?"

His gaze refocused on her. "Actually, I don't know. But he certainly wouldn't destroy his father's portrait and then ask me to waste everyone's time finding out who did it. See what else you can find out. If they're all swapping beds, at least they might provide alibis for each other."

He swung onto the horse just as a lady in a smart, dark blue riding habit walked into the yard.

"Mrs. Bramley," April muttered to his lordship and effaced herself.

She didn't like to think of him riding with the beautiful widow. Mainly because *she* wanted to be the one riding with him. He'd begun teaching her while they'd stayed at Haybury Court, his main seat. She couldn't do it here. In fact, even on his own estates, it was considered eccentric if not downright scandalous.

PIERS WONDERED IF HE would have recognized Mrs. Bramley if April hadn't warned him. Now that he had noticed her, he found her curiously familiar. He was even pleased to see her, and not just because of the information she might reveal.

"Good morning, my lord," she greeted him cheerfully, as the yawning groom led out her saddled mare. Using the block to mount, she gathered the reins efficiently, and trotted beside him onto the bridle path. "Who was that girl? She doesn't look like any of Irene's servants."

"She isn't. She is my assistant."

Mrs. Bramley's glance was expressionless. "Is she," she said without emphasis.

"A cross between a secretary and a dogsbody," said Petteril, giving her time to work out that a gentleman would not take a low-born mistress to a lady's house.

"It might start a new fashion for female secretaries," Mrs. Bramley said. "But she is far too pretty not to cause talk."

"People will always talk. Neither ignorance nor knowledge can prevent it. It is a beautiful morning."

"Indeed it is," she replied, though a moment later, she turned her head toward him, smiling. "You go your own way, do you not, my lord?"

"Don't you?"

She thought about it. "No, I am not brave enough. Like most of us to a greater or lesser degree, I am a prisoner of convention."

"I doubt that. I suspect you make a few concessions to convention that you might more easily do as you wish and still preserve the peace."

"How very perceptive of you," she said lightly.

"Is that why you surrendered so gracefully to Irene when she married Sir Weston?"

"No. I genuinely liked Irene. We were friends before any of us had ever met him."

He pounced. "Any of us? Do you include Mrs. Laughton, then?"

"Yes," she said boldly. "All three of us wished to marry him. But you already know that, don't you?"

"Was he faithful to Irene?" he asked, holding her gaze.

"Yes. At least, so far as I know. If he was unfaithful, he did so with commendable discretion. I don't wish to give you the wrong impression, my lord. I did not carry a torch for Sir Weston into my own marriage. I was afraid I might, but in fact, I loved my husband very much. Even had Weston been willing to indulge in a liaison, I would not."

"Is Mrs. Laughton so scrupulous?"

"She is less fortunate. I believe she took Laughton largely to make Weston jealous."

"Did it?"

A smile flickered and vanished. "No. He was happy with Irene, despite the difference in their ages."

"Mrs. Laughton is not...content, is she?"

"She is a restless soul, always looking for something she never finds."

"In a man?"

Mrs. Bramley tightened her reins to stop her mare lipping at passing leaves. For a few moments, she picked her way along the path in silence. Then she said, "Yes. She is one of those women who only defines herself through men."

"Do you think she genuinely loved Sir Weston?"

"I'm sure it was genuine to her. But you and I might not recognize it as such." As though sensing his surprise she cast him a rueful smile. "You find me cynical? Harsh? Others might call me perceptive."

"They might indeed. Tell me, if I were to ask you, could you prove your whereabouts from just before midnight on Tuesday until five o'clock on Wednesday morning?"

"No, though I was in the stables before six. If you are asking politely if I sleep alone or if I have a lover, then it is the former."

"Would you like to have a lover?"

Her eyes moved slowly to his, betraying laughter but behind that a crushing loneliness that spoke to his own. "Is that an invitation, my lord?"

"I would not be so gauche," he said lightly, although heat seeped into his cheeks and a physical longing into his more nether regions. "Perhaps I should rephrase the question. Would you think it disloyal or offensive for a widow to seek—er...consolation?"

"No. Would you?"

"Never having been widowed, I don't feel qualified to opine, although I am, generally speaking, in favour of happiness."

"Do you ever find it?"

Piers gazed between his horse's ears. "On occasion." Fleeting and elusive, even *illusive*. An image spun through his mind—April in a shaft of dusty sunlight through an attic window, dancing across the floor in borrowed clothes, with all the joy of a child dressing up. And all the beautiful curves of a woman. He blinked to banish the memory.

He wanted to ask Mrs. Bramley about Irene and St. Etienne, but he had the feeling she would not tell him. Instead, he approached the matter obliquely. "Has anyone pursued you, romantically speaking, since you came to Pelton Park this month?"

She laughed. "My dear sir, I am entirely eclipsed by the beauty of Irene and Susan Laughton. And by the joyous innocence of your delightful cousin."

She did not mention Marianne Orville.

"Which of them does Randal Hope pursue?" Piers asked.

"All of them and none. They are all mere notches on a bedpost to Hope. And I would not put it past him to ruin your little cousin just for the fun of it, so be warned."

"I am. What of Laughton?"

She sighed. "Laughton is too angry and too in love with his wife."

"What is he angry about?"

"That he is in love with his wife. So unfashionable, my dear."

Petteril smiled slightly. "And what of Monsieur St. Etienne?"

"I imagine he is too busy dodging Randal Hope's barbs and trying to paint Peter."

"Do you really imagine that?" he asked, meeting her gaze.

"You think because he is French, he must constantly have a lover?" she mocked.

"Well, he does not have a wife, nor, I understand, the means to support one. Would you commission him?"

"I might if I had any desire to be immortalised in oils, which I don't."

"Perhaps you should. Who else has he painted? Beside Sir Weston."

"Oh, lots of the ton in the past. Lady Jersey, Lord and Lady Sefton. Even the Laughtons."

His eyebrows shot up. "Then he knew them before he came to Pelton Park?"

"I expect Irene or Weston introduced him to them. Does it matter?"

"I don't know," Piers said, though for some reason he was sure it did. Something churned in his mind, trying to resolve itself into fact, or at least a theory.

"Why are you so interested?" she asked curiously. "Do you often try to solve such mysteries?"

"It does seem to happen more since I inherited the title," he admitted. "My previous mysteries tended to be academic. Or merely finding who boxed the watch at Oxford. Or who copied the essay from whom."

"But you choose to do it when it is not your responsibility. Why?"

"I suppose I must be bored," Piers said lightly, before he realized that he was not. He had not really been bored since the day he had dressed up as a forger and gone looking for April in the back streets of St. Giles. The thought made him smile and when Mrs. Bramley smiled back, he liked that too.

APRIL FOUND MISS DEAL, Lady Haggard's personal maid, pressing her mistress's clothes with a smoothing iron. Since Deal wasn't snooty like most ladies' maids, April went and asked humbly if she could help.

"Ever pressed clothes before?" Deal asked.

"No," April admitted. "But I like to learn."

"Maybe you should just watch me for a bit then."

"Thank you," April said. "I thought of trying to become a lady's maid once," she said, without mentioning the effort had been a ruse to get into a certain lady's private rooms to search them. "But I don't think I could work for most ladies. Me mouth's too big."

Deal smiled. "Knowing your faults is a start. But there's no denying a good mistress makes all the difference."

"You're lucky to work for Lady Haggard. She seems very kind."

"She is. You can't mess her around, mind, but you wouldn't want to. She's fair and I'm happy to work hard for her."

"That's the other thing about my big mouth," April confided, watching the iron glide to every corner of a chemise, even flattening out tapes and a touch of lace at the neck. "I wouldn't mean to be disloyal but once the words tumble out, I can't take 'em back, can I?"

"You mean gossiping about your mistress? There's some as do, but they won't last long in the position. Keeping your character is everything."

April, who had never had a "character", nodded sagely. "I can see that."

Deal put down the iron, quickly and neatly folded the chemise and handed it to April. "Put it on the pile for me."

April obliged. "What about when the mistress asks you for gossip about other people? Is that allowed?"

Deal was already ironing the next item—a pretty, lawn nightgown, with delicate embroidery. "Of course. It's your job to give her what she wants. So long as she understands you're not a gossip by nature."

"So, if one of the other maids wasn't as loyal as you and blabbed about her mistress, then you would tell Lady Haggard?"

"If she asked." She lifted her eyes from the night rail. "Something bothering you, April?"

April shook her head. "Oh no. Just trying to get things straight. I heard about a certain bed not being slept in and I thought how complicated it was what secrets to keep and what not."

Deal pursed her lips, folded the nightgown, and passed it to April before placing the iron on the stove behind her and picking up the other with a thick, cloth pad. "If you're talking about Mrs. Laughton's maid, I wouldn't say anything to anyone. They both live to cause trouble."

"Oh goodness, I'm glad I spoke to you. What about Mrs. Bramley?"

"A real lady. Never heard anything against her." Ironing another chemise, Deal threw her a sly look. "She's riding out with your Lord Petteril."

"Cor," April said admiringly. "Nothing much gets past you, does it?"

"No," Deal said. "So don't you forget it!"

WHEN DEAL ANSWERED her mistress's bell, April decided to go and see if the artist was at work. Emerging from the green baize door, she heard laughter coming from the main staircase.

A moment later, his lordship's little cousin Gussie appeared, rushing with her usual liveliness. She was dressed to go out in a very pretty blue bonnet and pelisse, but she did not move straight to the front door. As though waiting for someone, she wandered idly around the hall, looking at pictures.

To people of Gussie's station, servants were largely invisible. April walked past her without expectation of even being noticed let alone recognized. But Gussie, ever curious like her cousin, cast her a quick glance and then came back for another.

"Goodness, it's you again," she said in clear surprise. "I didn't know you were with Lady Haggard now."

"I'm not," April admitted, so surprised that she almost forgot to curtsey. "How are you, Miss Gussie?"

"Oh, well as always, thank you. Has my cousin brought his entire household with him?" Her eyes had begun to dance with amusement.

"No. The others have gone on to Sillitrees with the horses."

Gussie took a step nearer and lowered her voice. "You *are* that boy who was with the horses, aren't you?"

April grinned before she could help it. Part of her still longed to be that boy with the horses. "Don't be daft, miss. Do I look like a boy?"

Gussie looked her up and down. "No, you don't," she said frankly. "But then you're not much like a servant either. What's going on?"

"I'm helping his lordship find out who splattered paint all over Sir Weston's portrait."

Gussie's eyes widened, a hint of envy amidst the surprise.

April cast a quick glance around the hall, empty apart from the two of them. Even if someone was skulking behind a door, they shouldn't be able to overhear if she kept her voice down.

"Did you see anything odd on Tuesday night?" she asked Gussie.

"Odd?"

"People where they shouldn't be. Footsteps. Doors closing. That kind of thing."

"I thought it happened during the night."

"And you're always sound asleep during the night, ain't you? Never up and about looking for mischief."

"Never," Gussie said, dimpling.

"Pull the other one," April said. "It's got bells on."

"What?"

"Miss, help us out."

Gussie bent nearer. "You won't tell Mama?"

"Is she likely to speak to me?" April demanded.

"No, but Piers..."

"I don't *have* to tell his lordship," April said, crossing her fingers behind her back. "He don't need to know where the facts come from, just the facts themselves. If you got any."

"Well, not facts as such," Gussie said doubtfully. "But lots of people were up late. I was in the library playing chess until after two in the morning."

April blinked. "Chess?"

"You needn't sound so surprised," Gussie said with dignity. "I am very good at chess."

"I believe you. Who were you playing with?"

"Sir Peter and Mr. Orville. And then Mr. Hope came in, too."

"When did Hope come in?"

"Shortly after midnight, I think. He'd been playing billiards with Mr. Laughton. But Mr. Laughton went straight up to bed."

"Did you see him go?"

"Well, the door was open. I saw him walk up the stairs toward the bedchambers."

"And you played chess with all these gentlemen until after two o'clock?"

"We took turns at the board, but no one left the room until we all retired at the same time."

"Did anyone go downstairs? Did you hear anyone moving around after you retired?"

Gussie frowned. "I thought I heard the door next to mine open and close once, but I was very sleepy."

"Who sleeps in that room?"

"Mr. and Mrs. Laughton."

"Anything else?"

"Voices," Gussie said vaguely. "Further away."

"Men's voices? Women's?"

"Women's. I think."

"Before or after the Laughtons' door opened and closed?"

"After, I think. No, before. Maybe both. Or it might all have been part of my dreams."

"Who won the chess tournament?" April asked so suddenly that Gussie blinked.

"Mr. Orville. He is very good."

"Are the others?"

"Sir Peter isn't bad. Mr. Hope was more interested in me. Until I beat him and then Orville beat him twice. Now Mr. Hope wants to beat us both. He is very competitive by nature."

A sudden thought occurred to April. "Does St. Etienne play chess?"

"I have no idea."

"You didn't see him that night?"

"Not after we left the drawing room."

Footsteps hurrying down the stairs drew April's attention. Randal Hope, in perfect morning dress, hat in hand, strode toward them.

"Watch him," April breathed. "He ain't safe."

Gussie bestowed a kind smile upon her. "I know." She turned the smile upon Mr. Hope as she marched toward him. "There you are. I was about to go on my own."

Hope spared April no more than a flickering glance. His attention was clearly all on Gussie. Uneasily, April wondered if she should follow them to look after the girl. Seriously, after the Henry Devon affair, she should have developed some sense. And where was her wretched mother?

Chapter Six

Randal Hope was not a fortune hunter. He didn't need to be. His father was a wealthy man and Randal's allowance was generous enough to last him until he inherited everything. On the other hand, he wouldn't *mind* access to Gussie's dowry as well as to Gussie herself.

As she stepped outside on his arm, he reflected that she really was a taking little thing and for the first time he actually considered marrying her. He hovered between that and teaching her a useful and pleasurable lesson—one shouldn't play if one did not mean to pay. He could still marry her later if the notion didn't go off him.

That it might go off her never entered his head.

Most rakes of his acquaintance were too leary to touch unmarried ladies of gentle birth, frightened of being forced into marriage. Whereas Hope had discovered while still in his teens that they were just as easy to touch without repercussions because they were too ashamed to tell. Provided one didn't knock them up, of course.

Gussie blew so hot and cold that he really felt more tantalized than he ever had in his life before. He was not used to waiting and the novelty was wearing off.

"You are an odd little creature, are you not?" he said. "Does your mama *like* you to gossip with servants?"

"I never gossip," Gussie said grandly. "And of course we are brought up to care for our people."

"Is that girl *your people*?" he asked, curling his lip.

"Our people," Gussie corrected. "My family's."

"Your cousin Petteril's. Trust me, your mama would not approve. To be frank, I'm surprised Lady Haggard allows her in the house. She must be either naive or desperate."

"Don't be silly, Randal," Gussie said, clearly bored. "Not everyone bothers the maids."

He blinked at her, wondering if that shot was as sharp as it sounded. But she was not even looking at him. Instead, she waved, smiling at her cousin Petteril, who was just dismounting in the stable yard. In his company was Mrs. Bramley, who always made Randal feel like an importunate schoolboy. Even though, as an ageing widow, she should have been damned grateful for the attention.

But she was laughing up at Piers Withan, and her eyes were not indifferent at all.

"Good morning!" Gussie called. "We are just walking off our breakfast. Care to join us?"

Hope tried not to scowl, but really, she was damned annoying.

"Oh, we have ridden for miles!" Mrs. Bramley said. "And I'm afraid I am for my own breakfast, if there is any left."

"I shall join your walk," Petteril said, maddeningly, delivering his horse to the waiting groom. "Mrs. Bramley, thank you for your delightful company." He tipped his hat to the lady and fell into step beside Randal. "So where are we off to, Gussie?"

"Oh, just a ramble round the gardens. I shall have to be back when Mama emerges from her room."

"So shall I," Piers said. "I was hoping for a word with her. What are your plans for the day, Hope?"

"They are already in ruins if Miss Withan means to desert me so soon."

"Only for a little," Gussie assured him. "There is a treasure hunt this afternoon, remember."

"Joy unconfined," Randal muttered. "What are your plans, Petteril? Playing headmaster again and questioning all the boys?"

"Do you think I should?" Petteril said so blandly that Randal peered at him.

Randal had never understood Piers Withan. He had merely despised him. Or at least he thought he did. Randal was rarely unsure and he didn't like the feeling. He certainly did not like what Piers had grown into. The change was both dizzying and curiously inevitable. It all made him uncomfortable, and that made him angry.

"Very well," Piers said, as though doing him a favour. His eyes were not serious at all. Was the clunch actually mocking him? "Where were you in the early hours of Thursday morning?"

Randal saw his chance and smiled his best, dazzling smile. Gussie was walking away to accost to Sir Peter, which did not improve Randal's mood.

Leaning deliberately toward Petteril, he whispered in his ear. "Where was I? Ask your little cousin." And before the dolt could react, he walked away laughing.

He even whistled as he went. There was always some amusement to be had from life.

PIERS'S COUSIN GUSSIE was the only member of his surviving family for whom he was legally responsible. She was also the only one he felt any true fondness for.

It was time, past time, for another quarrel with her mother.

He did not like Hortensia, his uncle's widow. He had avoided her as a child, and since he had inherited the title, her unrelenting hostility wearied him. But needs must when the likes of Randal Hope were involved.

Rather than beard St. Etienne in his studio, which had been his original aim on returning from his ride, he passed his hat to the waiting footman who let him back into the house and said, "Thank you. Any idea where I might find Lady Petteril?"

"I believe her ladyship is in the drawing room, my lord."

"Thank you."

In the drawing room doorway, he almost collided with a lady coming out.

"Excuse me," he said, falling back at once.

But her gaze was both assessing and bold and not remotely annoyed. "The fault is mine for daydreaming, my lord."

That voice. It could turn a man inside out. Had he not other things on his mind.

Piers bowed to Mrs. Laughton. "Hardly, ma'am. I was the one rushing."

"My nephew is notoriously clumsy," Aunt Hortensia's voice said from within.

To his surprise, Mrs. Laughton smiled and patted his hand with a sympathy that was almost conspiratorial.

"Good luck," she breathed and walked gracefully away.

Piers brought his attention smartly back to the matter in hand. He went into the drawing room to discover his aunt alone, ensconced on a comfortable sofa with her needlework.

He closed the door behind him and bowed. "Aunt."

"Piers. Why have you closed the door?"

"Because I wish to speak to you in private and this seems a perfect opportunity."

"I cannot think what you have to say to me that may not be heard by all and sundry. Even if it would not interest them in the slightest."

"I know you cannot," he said, pulling up a chair opposite the sofa so that he sat near enough to speak quietly.

"Have you learned no manners?" Hortensia reared back against the sofa, her nostrils flaring with distaste. "A gentleman does not invade a drawing room smelling of the stables. Go and change at once."

"I shall in a moment," he said peaceably. "Aunt, are you aware Randal Hope is pursuing Gussie?"

"*Courting* Gussie," she corrected with some satisfaction. "And you are not to interfere and spoil her chances again, Piers."

Piers held her gaze. "Her chances of what? Ruin? Or mere misery?"

"Marriage," she retorted.

"Just the misery then. Are you even aware of his reputation?"

"Oh, don't be a stuffy old woman. Gentlemen will sow their wild oats. That will change when he marries."

Piers counted to five. "It might," he allowed. "But you should know that will not be to Gussie for at least a year."

Her lips slackened. She dropped her work into her lap. "A *year*? Have you lost whatever poor wits you were born with? She has had her first Season already! In a year she will be—"

"Eighteen. In a year she will be eighteen. Hardly an old crone."

"Missed chances never come back!"

"No, they don't. Have you forgotten Henry Devon already?"

"No, I have not," Hortensia flared. "Which is why I shall not tolerate your further interference in Gussie's life!"

"Who is interfering in my life?" Gussie enquired, tripping into the room.

"Close the door," snapped her mother. "Piers is, of course. He is pleased to disapprove of your choice—again!—and thinks he can prevent your marrying for an entire year!"

"Actually, he can prevent it for almost four," Gussie pointed out, sitting down on the other side of the sofa from her mother. "And to be honest, I am not likely to have the chance to marry very soon."

Hortensia glared at Piers. "What have you said to Randal Hope?"

"About Gussie? Nothing. Actually, it was he who mentioned her to me." He caught Gussie's sparkling eye. "He's a bit of a commoner, Gussie. A loose tongued scoundrel."

"I know," she said candidly.

Perhaps he liked her because she always managed to surprise him.

Her mother blinked rapidly, then sat up straight with triumph. "There! You see? Now go away and stop pestering her." Another idea clearly dropped into her mind and her jaw dropped. "Oh no! You think to marry her *yourself*? I won't have it!"

Gussie laughed.

"Neither will Gussie," Piers said dryly, although he was slightly alarmed to see the speculation in his cousin's face. "Seriously, don't be alone with Hope." In front of his aunt, he was reluctant to say more. So he rose, and with a last attempt to reach Hortensia, added, "Gussie's safety depends on you, aunt."

Hortensia sniffed. He was half way to the door before she said spitefully, "By the by, you should change your man of business. He is hopeless. He still has not provided the advance I requested two weeks ago."

It was depressing to fight the same battles over and over. He turned to face her. "There will be no advance, aunt. Your allowance is generous. You must wait until quarter day."

"And how do you expect us to live on nothing until then?"

Piers shrugged. "If you are truly short—which I doubt—sell a few jewels. Sell a painting." She could begin with one of those she had removed from Petteril House. He was unlikely to see them again anyway. "My man of business will help, if you pay his account."

"Miser!" Aunt Hortensia flung at his back as he closed the door.

In the passage, a liveried footman lurked near enough to have heard her outburst, so Piers refrained from smiling.

Instead, he said, "Will you send April to the library?"

The footman, who might have been the same one who had let him in a quarter of an hour ago, bowed and said, "Certainly, my lord." His eyes were wintry, and when he turned on his heel, something in his manner spoke of insolence and dislike.

Perhaps Piers needed to pay a visit to the servants' hall. Or at least have another word with the butler. Thoughtfully, he ran upstairs to change and five minutes later opened the door to the library. He was glad to find it empty.

April breezed in a few moments later. "Whatcher, mister?"

"Not much cheer at all," he said ruefully, turning from the window. "Leave the door and come over here."

"What we looking at?" she asked, obeying.

"Nothing. I don't want the rest of the household to hear us. Does that footman I sent for you listen at doors?"

"William?" she said in surprise. "I shouldn't think so. He seems decent. Maybe he's trying to find out stuff—same as you and me."

"Maybe," Piers said, shaking off the issue for now. "Learn anything to help us rule anyone out of suspicion?"

"Yes, but you ain't going to like it," April warned. "Four of 'em were in here playing chess until after two in the morning."

"Which four?"

April marked them off on her fingers. "Hope, Orville, Haggs—I mean Sir Peter—and – er..." She dropped her hands to her sides. "Miss Gussie."

"Gussie?" He stared at her.

April, clearly uneasy, gave a rueful shrug of her shoulders.

"The little minx," Piers said softly. "So *that* is what she is up to."

"What?" April demanded.

"She doesn't want to marry Hope. No wonder she was not remotely bothered when she learned I would not countenance it. She's flirting with him to try and make someone else jealous."

"Who?" April asked.

"I could hazard a guess, but it's someone with principles, for she knows he wouldn't marry her within the year."

"One of the chess players. Orville? My money's on Sir Peter."

"So is mine, or the hussy would never have inveigled my aunt to bring her to a party with so few eligible young men present. That is not my worry. She is too sure of herself."

"But she knows the dangers," April said unexpectedly. "She'll be careful."

"Wouldn't it be comfortable," Piers murmured, "to be able to send Hope away for defacing his host's property?"

"Do you think he did it?"

"Actually, he is one of the few I find unlikely. I can see no motive for him, unless it was merely to annoy St. Etienne."

"Because he's French and not born a gentleman? Wouldn't Hope despise him too much to bother?"

"Probably. Unless he was drunk and reverted to schoolboy pranks. I can't say he has grown up much."

Her eyebrows lifted. "I forgot you knew him before."

"We were at school together, though he was a couple of years ahead of me."

"What was he like? A bully?"

"Yes."

Her eyes narrowed. "He pick on you?"

"No, he barely noticed my existence until he began to—er...pick on a friend of mine."

"Did you help stand up to him?" April asked eagerly.

"Not exactly," Piers murmured. "I distracted him."

"How?"

"Did his work for him."

April scowled. "That ain't right."

"No, but it got him off poor Sam's back and earned us a fair bit of money besides. All his idiot friends bid for our services, too."

"But you must have been up all night working!"

"Only took a few minutes each. Couldn't do it too well or the masters would have smelled a rat."

"Ain't he ashamed to look you in the eye now?" April said indignantly.

"No, that's the thing," Piers said. "He still thinks I'm the fool, though I ended up with most of his allowance and half his tuck. I think he is far too self-absorbed to know the difference between right and wrong."

"So, he wouldn't care enough to damage the painting?"

"I could be mistaken."

"Wish you were."

April took out her notebook, flipping the pages to her most recent notes. Piers was proud to see the letters more neatly formed than ever. She still practiced every day, wherever they were.

"The chess players all retired at the same time—safety in numbers for Miss Gussie though her ma would have had a fit anyhow. But there was movement in the house after two o'clock. She half-woke to hear the door next to hers opening and closing, and there were women's voices further away."

"Women's?" he said with interest. "Ladies or servants?"

"I don't think she could tell. Unlikely to be servants before five in the morning, though. They're all too knackered to run about the house gossiping. Out like a light, they are."

"Which leaves Lady Haggard, Mrs. Bramley, Mrs. Laughton and my aunt."

"Mr. and Mrs. Laughton sleep in the room next to Miss Gussie's. Lady P's on her other side."

"The Laughtons don't have separate rooms?"

"You're surprised. Don't they like each other?" she asked.

"Not much. Or at least I doubt she is over-enamoured with him. Apparently, she carried a torch for Sir Weston. St. Etienne painted their portraits too."

Her eyebrows flew up. "Did he? When?"

"Not long after he painted Sir Weston's, I think. But it means they knew him before they came here."

"Interesting," she allowed.

Piers agreed. He let the ideas whirl around his brain for a bit, then refocused to find April gazing at him. Disconcerted, he blinked at her.

"Got an idea?" she asked hopefully.

"Someone blinded Sir Weston—symbolically speaking—so that he would not see something. Something he would have cared about and disliked. I think I need to speak to Mrs. Laughton."

"And Mr. Laughton if he'll snitch on her." Her eyes gleamed. "I think we might be getting close to the truth."

Chapter Seven

"Do me a favour, Haggs," Piers murmured as he walked outside with his friend to begin the treasure hunt. "See that Gussie is not paired with Hope."

"Your wish is my command," Haggs said so flippantly that Piers knew he had already decided. "Any particular partner you wish to choose for yourself?"

"Mrs. Laughton."

"A fine choice," said Haggs. "Though Irene had you paired with Jane Bramley."

It came to him that this would have pleased him more. But it was Susan Laughton he needed to speak to.

As everyone emerged with varying degrees of excitement and boredom, Lady Haggard gathered them around her.

"The bad news, my friends," she said gaily, "is that I shall not be playing, since I placed all the clues and the treasures. I am also responsible for the teams, so you may thank me later. Lady Petteril, you are with Mr. Orville. Miss Withan is with Peter, Mrs. Bramley with Mr. Hope, Miss Orville with Mr. Laughton and, last but not least. Mrs. Laughton with Lord Petteril."

"Is St. Etienne not joining us?" Piers asked.

"Alas no, he is setting to work repairing my husband's portrait before he begins on Peter's. Now, I shall give each of you a starting place where you will find your first clues. Follow them to the treasure if you can, and if and when you find it, rush back here."

She gave each of the gentlemen a small scrap of paper. While she did so, Piers found his arm taken in a proprietary grip.

"My lord," said that warm, smooth voice that could probably have seduced a monk. "What good fortune for me since I understand you are the puzzle solver in chief! Where are we to begin?"

"The old oak at the edge of the west wood," he read.

"Where in the world is that?"

"Not far," said Piers, who remembered it well enough to know that Haggs and not his stepmother had planned that part of the game.

APRIL DISCOVERED CLAUDE St. Etienne in his studio, using some evil-smelling solution to remove the ugly black "blindfold" from Sir Weston's portrait. If he was aware of her entrance, he gave no sign of it, merely carried on working.

"Ain't you afraid of taking off the paint underneath, too?" she asked at last.

"Yes. So don't disturb me."

"Sorry." April perched on a nearby stool to watch in silence until he lifted his hand and stood back to assess his progress. A small patch of black beside the head had vanished. "I thought you'd just paint over the top of it."

"Too thick, too black, wrong texture."

"Fair enough," April said meekly. "You work very neat, sir," she added, as he searched for a clean patch of rag. "I don't imagine you leave everything lying around when you finish in the evening."

He gave her a withering look.

"I mean," she explained, "whoever did that to the picture must have dug out the paint and used a brush. He didn't just *throw* paint at it, did he?"

"Everything was put away," St. Etienne said repressively.

"Course it was. Was it out next morning when you discovered the damage?"

He stared at her. "No." He waved one hand toward the open chest on the table beside him. "Everything was in there where I'd put it. Even the brush had been cleaned."

"That's weird," April said. "Who'd do that to a painting and then bother to clean up?"

"Someone who wanted to put the blame on me," St. Etienne said bitterly.

"'Cause you're French?"

He shrugged irritably, dipped the rag in his stinking solution and moved it toward Sir Weston's face. He was frowning ferociously.

"Who else you paint then? Among these people." She waved a vague hand toward the open window and terrace from where laughing voices drifted. "Mrs. Bramley?"

"No. Only Mr. and Mrs. Laughton." His unsteady hand dropped to his side once more. With the other, he rubbed furiously at his forehead. "What do you want, anyway? Go and do your own work and stop interrupting mine."

April jumped off her stool, smiled and left the room to find Cheryl the maid, to see if she had cleaned any brushes before she noticed the damage to the portrait and legged it.

She had.

SUSAN LAUGHTON TURNED out to be amusing company, sharp of eye and mind. She found the first clue at the old oak and worked it out almost as fast as Piers.

"It must have taken Irene ages," Mrs. Laughton observed idly as they walked toward the lake. "To arrange all this, make all the clues and plant them."

"Clearly, she takes her duties as a hostess seriously. You have been friends a long time, have you not?"

"Yes, I suppose we have now. I was really Weston's friend first."

He looked at her. "But you must have been much younger than Sir Weston."

She laughed, a soft and husky sound. "A few years. His first wife was a family friend." She tilted her chin and met his gaze. "And yes, before you ask, I was in love with Weston. From the moment I met him until the day he died. But Irene made him happy. I shall always be grateful to her for that."

He regarded her. "That is a very selfless love."

"Isn't it?" she said flippantly. "I surprise myself sometimes. You are right, of course. I am not a selfless person. But Sir Weston meant the world to me."

"Why?" Piers asked curiously.

"I don't know. Some men just have that...something. One cannot always lay one's finger on what it is, but one always recognizes it." She glanced up at him through the ringlets of her elegant little fringe. "You have it, too. In an entirely different way."

"I do?" he said, startled.

She laughed and took his arm. "Perhaps *that* is why. You take nothing and no one for granted, do you, my lord?"

"I don't know," he said uncomfortably, glad to see the lake glistening between the trees. "Are you tired? Shall we sit for a little by the lake? I recall there being stone benches around it."

"Excellent idea. So long as it does not make us lose the treasure!"

"You like to win?" he asked idly.

"Don't you?"

"In my own way, perhaps."

"Solving puzzles is your form of victory?" she said, settling with a sigh on the curved stone bench at the edge of the lake.

He sat beside her, half-turned toward her. "One of them. Will you help me solve this mystery of Sir Weston's portrait?"

"I will try," she answered without hesitation. "What can I do?"

"Tell me about Claude St. Etienne."

She smiled. "He is French."

"Is that all? Is he not a talented painter?"

"I think so. I liked his portrait of Weston."

"What of his portrait of you and your husband?"

"Not quite so good. He flattered us both just a little too much."

"Why would he do that for you more than for Sir Weston?"

She met his gaze with lazy amusement though behind that was a hint of defiance that was not remotely child-like. "I like to think because he was in love with me at the time. And because he felt guilty about Matthew. My husband."

"Am I to imagine you and St. Etienne formed a liaison?"

"You already know we did," she said frankly. "Or you would not be asking me such questions."

"How did such a liaison fit with your great love for Sir Weston?" he wondered.

Her smile was twisted. "I said Claude was in love with me, not I with him. As a man, you must be aware of the differences between love and mere pleasure."

Piers shifted position but held her gaze. "Have you resumed your liaison with St. Etienne since coming to Pelton Park?"

"Sleeping in the same room as my husband? Don't be silly."

"Does he know?"

"About Weston or Claude?"

"Both."

Her fingers began to pleat at the fabric of her skirts. "He always knew about Weston—all there was to know. Weston never touched me, you know, even before he married Irene. He was far too much the gentleman. I have no idea what Matthew knew about Claude and me. It's not important."

Her gaze fell from his to her restless fingers and she seemed to force them to stillness.

"In the small hours of Wednesday morning, before anyone discovered the damage to the portrait, did you hear women's voices in the passage near your bedchamber?"

Her gaze lifted to his. "My, you are busy, are you not? Yes, I heard them. One of them was mine. I went to talk to Irene."

"In the middle of the night?"

"Why not since we were both awake?"

"What did you talk about?"

She smiled, very faintly, with a mere hint of mockery. "Oh, life and love. Women's chatter."

"Do you think Irene is in love?"

"Do you think I won't tell her you asked me such a thing? Ask her yourself."

"I will," Piers said, rising to his feet. "Shall we search out this loose stone?"

THE TREASURE HUNT WAS won by Randal Hope and Mrs. Bramley.

"I thought you were supposed to be the clever one," Hope mocked Piers as he fastened the treasure—a rather beautiful antique gold bracelet—around Mrs. Bramley's arm.

"Who told you that?" Piers wondered, turning to the lady. "Mrs. Bramley, my compliments!"

Since the weather was still lovely, tea was again served on the terrace. Piers had no real opportunity to speak to anyone privately, but he found himself watching Haggs's cousin, Kenneth Orville, who was so civilly attentive to Aunt Hortensia that Piers could not help being impressed by his endurance. He must have been a hostess's dream guest. On the other hand, he was the first to leave the terrace, claiming he had a sermon to write before Sunday.

Gussie flirted impartially with all the gentlemen, though never beyond what was pleasing. Piers wondered if she had taken his warning seriously. More likely, it was her chat with April that had made the difference.

As everyone else drifted inside the house, so did Piers. He went to his own chamber and dealt with correspondence that had followed him from London. That done, he pushed back his chair, swinging it onto its back legs while he thought about Sir Weston and the devotion he inspired and what the man would have least liked to see in his own home.

An answer offered itself to him, but he could not be sure.

Rising at last, he franked his letters and took them down to the front hall where a few others already waited to be collected for the post. He thought about going to the library, but realized he was merely putting off an unpleasant task.

Sighing, he set his foot on the first step and then caught sight of Yates, the butler, emerging from the baize door. His odd, stooped gait was unmistakeable. Piers waited until he was within discreet hailing distance.

"Would you ask Lady Haggard if she can spare me a few moments of her time?"

"Certainly, my lord."

"I'll wait in the library until she is free," Piers said.

He hoped to catch Orville there, but the man was clearly working in his own room, for the library was empty. Piers looked at the books instead, though it wasn't long before Yates reappeared.

"Her ladyship will receive you in her sitting room, my lord. Follow me, if you please."

Lady Haggard's rooms were at the corner of the same passage where his own chamber was located. In the still of night, Gussie might well have heard voices drifting from there.

When Yates knocked, it was Deal who opened the door and announced, "Lord Petteril, my lady."

"Thank you. You may go, Deal."

Piers entered and bowed while the servants effaced themselves. "I hope I am not disturbing you."

"Of course not. Please sit down." She rose from the desk where she had been writing letters, and came toward him, indicating the grouping of a sofa and two chairs by the empty fireplace. "Would you care for tea? Or sherry, perhaps?"

"No, thank you." When she was seated in one of the chairs, he sank onto the sofa opposite.

But now that he was here, facing her friendly, inquiring eyes, he found it difficult to begin. This was a whole new realm of awkwardness, and he had no easy role to fall into in order to deal with it.

This beautiful lady had been kind to him when he had been a gangly, inventive youth in his first year at Oxford, sprung on her without warning by her stepson. And several times after that. She had seemed to admire rather than deride his studious nature and talking to her had been easy.

"Have you learned anything important about the portrait?" she asked encouragingly.

He met her gaze and knew simple honesty was the only possible way forward. "Yes, I think so. But before I explain my theory and hurl accusations, I must ask you to confirm a few facts. I hope you understand that I regard everything you say to me in complete confidence."

Her eyes widened slightly but did not fall before his gaze. "Of course."

"You and Mrs. Laughton and Mrs. Bramley were once rivals, I understand, to be the second Lady Haggard."

She smiled slightly. "So they imagined. In reality, Weston never considered either of them as a wife. He loved me and knew that despite the difference in our ages, I loved him."

"None of that detracts from their feelings for him, however misguided, however little based on knowledge or reality."

"Perhaps not. What does this have to do with Weston's portrait?"

Piers pressed his thumbs together in his lap. "The night it was damaged, did you and Mrs. Laughton have a private conversation? At first in the passage and then in here?"

Wariness entered her expression, but she nodded.

"Could you tell me the precise times you encountered her and when she left you?"

"It must have been almost three when we met in the passage. She left about half an hour later. Is it important?"

"Yes, I think so. Was she upset when she left you?"

She lifted one hand as though to dismiss the idea, then let it fall into her lap. "A little, perhaps. I took it for her usual drama—she thrives on excitement and theatrics and I am afraid my mind was on other things."

"On Claude St. Etienne?"

Still her gaze met his. Only the sudden flush beneath her flawless skin betrayed discomfort. The silence stretched.

"You were right," she said. "You *have* learned things I would rather you did not."

"We are speaking in confidence," he reminded her. "And I have no right and less desire to judge you. Had Susan Laughton discovered your liaison with St. Etienne?"

Her shoulders sagged. "I think she suspected. That night I went to his chamber, but he was suffering one of his migraines and had taken a powder which let him sleep. I left him and then almost bumped into Susan in the passage." She waved one unsteady hand to the door. "She knew where I had been. I brought her in here to calm her down. She was...jealous."

"Did you know she had once had an affaire with St. Etienne?"

She smiled unhappily. "Susan does not keep such matters to herself. But she does not understand Claude any more than she understood Weston. Claude does not love either of us. He loves his art, but he needs human companionship, human passion." She closed her eyes and whispered. "So do I."

"Everyone does."

Her eyes opened, searching his. They lightened. "I believe you understand. And yet you contrive to appear so...unworldly. You are not, are you?"

He was asking so much of her, he had to give something back. "I recognize loneliness."

"Susan does not. She has a husband who adores her and she has her lovers. And yet to her I am the traitress. I have betrayed her and Weston with Claude."

Piers sighed with sheer relief. "I think, for her, Sir Weston was on a pedestal, and because he had chosen you, so were you, until you—er...fell off. I think that when she left you, she did not return to bed but went down to St. Etienne's studio and in an excess of emotion, she blacked out the portrait's eyes."

Lady Haggard stared at him. "It was symbolic. Implying that Weston should not see my fall from grace. While hoping everyone else would."

"Perhaps. I doubt her anger lasted long, and she probably felt ashamed of defacing his picture. Certainly, she has never admitted it."

Lady Haggard threw her head back as though in sudden pain. "When did she tell you about me and Claude? Do you suppose she has told Peter?"

He raised his brows. "She did not tell me. I rather guessed from your tired eyes and the way you avoid each other in public and yet seem so comfortable together."

"Unworldly," she murmured ruefully. "Your aunt has no idea about you, has she?"

Or about anything else. "She lost too much too quickly to be comfortable with me in the place her son should have inherited from her husband."

"You are generous."

"Only on the surface. So you believe I have a reasonable theory?"

"About the portrait? All too reasonable. I wish I had your powers of observation. I never thought she would do something so dramatic and then not remain at the centre of it all. She must indeed have been ashamed."

"Or I could be wrong," Piers admitted. "I would not confront her just yet—if such is your intention. I would be more comfortable making such an accusation if we could discover exactly when she returned to bed. I need to speak to Laughton."

Lady Haggard blinked. "And ask him to confirm he is a cuckold? Which is what he will think if Susan was away half the night."

"But she was—largely if not entirely—with you. I'll find a way." He rose to his feet, hesitated, then said merely, "Thank you."

She rose with him. "Have you told Peter?" she asked with difficulty.

He shook his head. "No. Remember, at this stage, Mrs. Laughton's guilt is only a theory, as is her motive." And perversely, now that Irene had confirmed so much of that theory, he began to see the flaws in the rest. Or perhaps he just wanted to.

"I don't want him to think I betrayed his father's memory," Lady Haggard said.

"Peter understands more than you give him credit for." And unlike everyone else, while he had loved his father he had also seen his flaws. He had never hero-worshipped him like everyone else.

"I hope so," she said hoarsely.

Chapter Eight

"I suppose you have Petteril in your sights now," Matthew Laughton said to his wife as they changed for dinner.

Susan sighed. "Because I was partnered with him for the treasure hunt? Does that mean little Marianne Orville is in yours?"

"She is a child," Laughton said impatiently. "Not even out. She is so shy she barely speaks."

"I thought that would be an attraction for you, since apparently I never stop."

He met her gaze in the mirror. "And what attracts you, Susan? Any man but me?"

"I have some standards," she mocked. "It is so unfashionable to be attracted only to one's husband."

"Under no circumstances must we offend the gods of fashion," he said savagely, and dropped his cuff link on the floor. Swearing beneath his breath, he bent and retrieved it.

When he straightened he found Susan right in front of him. Wordlessly, she took the sleeve button from his fingers and threaded it through his cuff.

"You are my husband," she said quietly. "I will always stand by you." She closed her fingers around his hand, raising her eyes to his. "That is the importance of marriage. We stand by each other."

For once, his entire attention seemed to be focused on her rather than on his own feelings. His eyes were unexpectedly perceptive. Almost like Petteril's, though thankfully not quite.

"What have you done?" he asked.

SINCE SHE LIKED TO be busy and she had not given up hope of learning more, April helped the Haggards' servants to set the table for dinner and fetched and carried the best serving dishes to the kitchen, ready to receive Cook's delicious-smelling offerings.

That done, she slipped out and made for the stairs.

"Where are you going?" William demanded behind her.

He filled the kitchen doorway and he was scowling.

"To see his lordship, of course."

"He hasn't rung for you."

"I still want to know if he needs anything."

William's eyes flashed. He took a step nearer her. "You can't go to his room!"

"Don't you tell me what I can't do," she retorted before the full implications of the accusation hit her. Heat flooded up from her toes. Most of it was anger. "I thought you were different. But you're just like everyone else, thinking the worst of him and blaming me for doing my job, which is just as respectable as yours, William High and Mighty, just not so boring."

She whirled around, nose in the air and stalked up the stairs.

"April, don't be like that," he said urgently. "I'm sorry. You got no one else to look out for you."

"I look out for myself. Always have, so bugger off!"

Fuming, she almost slammed through the servants' door on the first floor. Fortunately, the passage beyond was empty. Remembering to keep a weather eye open for trouble, she hurried along to the library door, which was partially open. She paused outside it, listening, then, hearing nothing, walked in.

Only Lord Petteril was present. Resplendent in evening dress, his long legs stretched under a table, he had a chess board beside him and a book open in front of him which he appeared to be reading with the aid of one of his quizzing glasses.

He glanced up. "April." The glass fell back onto his chest as she stormed into the room. "What has happened?"

"Nothing," she spat, throwing herself into the chair opposite. Then, "Bloody William! He had the nerve—the damn cheek—to order me not to go to your room."

Lord Petteril blinked. "Were you going to?"

"Of course I bloody wasn't! I ain't stupid!"

"No, but you are loud and swearing like a trooper."

Her eyes fell before his. "Sorry," she muttered. "Makes me mad."

"I know. But you can't be surprised."

"No. But I thought he understood. I thought he liked me." She risked a glance up at him and found his eyes fixed on her face. His pain caught at her breath, causing a surge of wonder. But perhaps it was just the sun beaming through the window, for when she blinked he looked as he always did.

"It's probably *because* he likes you that he is trying to look after you," he said.

She thought about that and found it didn't displease her. On the other hand, some things were unforgivable. "Well, he ain't looking after *you* to say such things."

"I look after myself too," he said gravely.

She smiled. "No you don't, mister. That's also my job."

"Leg it, scamp," he murmured, and she suddenly realized someone else was approaching the library.

She sprang up so fast she almost knocked her chair over. Beetling toward the door, she paused only to bob a curtsey to the newcomer, Mr. Orville, who, from all accounts below stairs, was a gentle and decent gentleman who owed much to the Haggards' kindness.

"Orville," Petteril said genially from the table. "I hear you play chess."

"DO YOU PLAY, MY LORD?" Orville replied with such surprise that Piers assumed either Hope or his aunt had been talking about him.

"I enjoy the odd game," Piers said. "I was hoping to have a quick one before dinner, and I understand you are the prevailing champion."

"Only because Sir Peter does not take it seriously," Orville said modestly.

He sat down in the chair April had just vacated and Piers pushed the board, already set up with its pieces, into the middle of the table. Picking up a black and a white pawn he rolled them between his hands and without looking, hid one in each fist. Orville tapped his right hand and was given the white pawn.

Piers turned the board. "You *do* take chess seriously?"

"I prefer to do my opponent the courtesy of keeping my mind on the game."

"Let me guess." Piers brought out his pawn to face Orville's. "Hope's and Sir Peter's attention was distracted by my little cousin Gussie. My only surprise is that she did not win overall."

"She beat both of them at least once."

"But not you?"

"As I said, my mind was on the game. And she had not the benefit of having been taught by Sir Weston."

"Of course. You are Sir Peter's cousin, are you not?"

"My mother was Sir Weston's sister. Sir Weston was my godfather and happily let my sisters and I run tame here over many a summer. In fact, I owe him my living at St. Claire's."

"Is that near here?"

"Near enough to visit. I shall return tomorrow, though my sister will remain with Lady Haggard for another week."

For a little, they played on in silence. Then Piers said, "I have been impressed by how well everyone here speaks of the late Sir Weston."

"He was an extraordinary man. I would even say a great one—a rich man who used his wealth and position for the benefit of others. There was nothing high in the instep about him, always willing to help and to understand."

From which Piers gathered that Orville's own parents were not. Taking a wild guess, he said, "Your own father did not understand your vocation for the Church?"

Orville grimaced. "My father was a soldier, sir, and understood no other way of life for a man." He blinked as Piers took his bishop. Then brought back his rook to protect his king and queen. "I shall always be grateful to Uncle Weston for supporting me in my desire to enter the Church. Without him, my father would never have countenanced it. But that is not why I hold my uncle in such affection."

Piers let him think and play his way out of the dilemma he had caused on the board, then gave him another. "You must have been very shocked by the defacement of his portrait."

Frowning at the board, Orville's attention, clearly, was only partly on the conversation. "Appalled, sir. Appalled. Such mindless violence—"

"Do you think it was mindless?" Piers asked, allowing surprise into his voice.

Orville blinked several times at the board. "Of course. There is no reason in such an act of vandalism."

"Not a terribly sensible one, I agree. But we are all subject to moments of temper or outrage where we might act against our better judgement."

"Speak for yourself," Orville said, snatching up Piers's queen.

"Check," Piers murmured and Orville slowly replaced it, frowning at Piers's bishop beyond. "Mate, I think. You have so much else to worry about, I expect your mind was not on the game."

JUST FOR A MOMENT, Orville felt his ears sing, as though the world was about to crash around him. Not because he had been beaten at chess—he knew he was good but he was hardly the finest player in the county—but because Lord Petteril seemed to see right through him.

And yet he had such an amiable face, humorous, even vague, except for those suddenly piercing dark eyes...

"Tell me," said his tormentor, "is your bedchamber on the family side of the house?"

"Of course. Next to Peter's."

"Then just across the hall from Lady Haggard's. The night the portrait was damaged and you played chess until late, were you disturbed even later by voices in the passage?"

"I fell asleep almost at once."

"That wasn't what I asked you."

Orville sprang to his feet. "I deny your right to ask me anything at all! You are impertinent, sir."

"You know what I have been commissioned to do," Petteril said quietly.

Orville closed his eyes. "By that woman," he said between his teeth.

For a long time, Petteril said nothing. Orville had to open his eyes to make sure he was still in the room.

"That woman," his lordship said in his soft, unemphatic voice, "is a lonely widow who has shown you nothing but kindness. Where is *your* Christian charity?"

Shame curled up from Orville's toes. "You are right," he whispered. "The shame is mine. You know, don't you?"

"I would rather hear the truth from you."

"I was so angry," he whispered, burying his face in his hands. "I heard them, Irene and Mrs. Laughton. I heard what they talked about, about Irene's vile liaison and her friend's pathetic jealousy. I could not be still. I found myself in the studio, without any memory of how I got there, gazing at Uncle Weston's portrait, painted by that treacherous Frenchman...!" He snatched a breath. "It was foolish. I threw open the chest, found the black paint and slathered it over his eyes. I wanted St. Etienne to know he was rumbled, to leave, preferably. But it was foolish, and it is I, not he, who is shamed." He shuddered and his voice dropped to a hoarse whisper. "How could I have done such a thing?"

Piers rose to his feet. "You are no more a saint than Sir Weston was. You could settle, as he did, for being a good man. Admit what you did and apologise. I think you will find she understands."

"DID SHE?" APRIL ASKED when Piers had told her everything in the stable yard that evening. Having fed the greys half a carrot each, she had been eager to hear his news.

"I don't think he's had the chance to speak to her. She has organized a musical evening for our entertainment this evening. Gussie and Miss Orville are hogging the limelight."

"Have you told her? Lady Haggs?"

"Only to murmur *en passant* that the culprit is not Susan Laughton."

"What put you on to Orville then? I'd never have pegged him."

"Nor I until this afternoon. He's a clergyman and appears much too mild ""mannered and devoted. What made me think again was something Lady Haggard said when I told her my suspicions about Mrs. Laughton. She said, *I never thought she would do something so dramatic and then not remain at the centre of it all. She must indeed have been ashamed.* She was right. Such an act for such a reason might fit Mrs. Laughton's dramatic flare but not her character. And she did not seem remotely ashamed to me."

"You were right, though, about it being personal and all about devotion to Sir Weston."

"Hero worship," Piers said ruefully. Solving this mystery brought little sense of relief, let alone triumph. Human nature might be fascinating, but it could also be damnably depressing. "Devotion without acknowledging any of the man's faults. Last night, when he spoke of Sir Weston, there was an almost fanatical look in his eyes. He never deferred to Haggs and barely looked at Lady Haggard. The odd time he did, I could not interpret his expression. I wondered if it was shame at wishing the poor soul a life of lonely widowhood after the great Sir Weston. In fact, I discounted him as the perpetrator, being a clergyman and perhaps too young and untried to be much use to his flock, however conscientious. Until Irene said *She must indeed have been ashamed.* She wasn't. But Orville was."

"Silly fool," April said cheerfully as they rounded the corner into the kitchen garden. "Does that mean we're leaving and going on to Sillitrees?"

"That was the plan. We can leave early tomorrow. I'd better get back to the drawing room. In you go."

With a quick grin over her shoulder, she took off toward the kitchen door at a run, like a gambolling puppy caught up in its mistress's clothes. She always made him smile.

Turning back, he walked around the house toward the side door he had left by. He did not really want to return to the party in the drawing room. In fact, he longed for solitude—not a simple matter since becoming the viscount, but at least at Sillitrees he would not be obligated by a host.

He re-entered the house and ambled toward the staircase. Although it was not quite dusk, lights blazed from the room St. Etienne used as his studio. On impulse, Piers changed direction and wandered in.

St. Etienne, a long, paint-spattered smock over his evening clothes, stood by the easel, a paintbrush in one hand, a wooden palette in the other. Beside him, on the floor, propped up against the table leg was the damaged portrait of Sir Weston, now with both eyes uncovered.

"Go away," St. Etienne said. "I am busy."

"So I see." Piers compromised by keeping a reasonable distance but continued to gaze at the artist's painting of Sir Peter Haggard. Already, it was easily recognizable. Haggs's face stared out of the canvas directly at Piers, with all the vitality and sardonic humour of his character blazing in his harsh, almost ugly features. The expression was so much Haggs that it caught at Piers's breath. But more than that, something about the angle of his stance spoke of vulnerability. The movement of his hands reaching for something unseen implied both practicality and constant endeavour.

"That is...wonderful," Piers said hoarsely.

"It might even be my masterpiece," St. Etienne said without pausing. His brush swiped busily about the background, "if I don't mess it up. A pity he is not someone more important. A great statesman or a soldier."

"You could not paint a statesman like that. It would not work half so well."

The brush stilled. St. Etienne spared him a glance, even the flicker of a smile. "You are right, of course. Not just a pretty face, as they say in England. I will paint you next, if there is time."

"Sadly, I shall be leaving tomorrow."

St. Etienne grunted and turned back to his portrait, assessing. "Lady Haggard thought you would. She will miss you. But at least she keeps the assistant."

Piers blinked. "What?"

"She makes the girl her secretary. Now you have given her the idea, she likes it. Is best for everyone."

Did he mean Lady Haggard liked it? Or April? He slammed the shutters on the desolation that threatened so suddenly. If it was true April had changed her mind, it was the best thing for her and he would damned well be happy for her. If it was not true, then nothing had changed. Either way, it was out of his hands right now.

"Not joining us in the drawing room?" he said, already making rather blindly for the door.

"No. I am busy."

THE WORDS DRIFTING from St. Etienne's studio filled William with triumph.

"...I shall be leaving tomorrow."

"Lady Haggard...miss you. But at least she keep the assistant... She makes the girl her secretary...best for everyone."

He was so thrilled, his hopes galloping far ahead of his knowledge, that he did not even have time to efface himself before the viscount came striding out of the room. Fortunately, Lord Petteril didn't appear to see him. He looked...stunned.

Serves him right, William thought, cock-a-hoop. Lords weren't used to losing the girl, but in this case, it seemed the mere third footman had won.

William wanted to shout and sing. Instead, he almost bolted back to the servants' hall in search of April.

Chapter Nine

In the drawing room, Lady Haggard and Marianne Orville were playing a clearly rehearsed duet on the pianoforte. Gussie sat on the sofa beside Randal Hope, while her mother sat on the other side of the room.

Orville, looking oddly blank, sat at the back, as though not even one of the party, though as Piers passed him, he caught at his sleeve.

"I can't do it this evening," he said miserably. "I'd never say all I need to. I shall depart early tomorrow and leave a letter for her explaining everything. *Confessing* everything. That way, she can cut me off if she wishes without embarrassment. Is it enough?"

"Is it enough for you?" Piers countered, even as he realized anything more was beyond the man right now.

There was no opportunity to speak to Lady Haggard with any privacy, so when he accepted a cup of tea from her hands, he said only, "I see St. Etienne is totally absorbed in Peter's portrait."

Lady Haggard beamed. "Isn't it wonderful?"

Haggs, who had overheard, walked with him toward the darkened window, saying uneasily, "Have you seen it? Is it awful?"

"The portrait? Actually, I think it's going to be brilliant."

"He'd rather paint you, you popinjay."

"Fortunately, I'm off tomorrow."

"You are? What about the defaced portrait?"

"You'll know tomorrow."

"I hate it when you're mysterious."

"I am an open book. Ask my aunt." Inclining his head politely to the glaring dowager, he turned back to Haggs, yawning, and drained his tea. "I am far too tired for any kind of explanation. I believe I shall have an early night."

"You should stay another day. We're having a dinner party tomorrow evening, with additional guests and dancing afterward."

Piers shuddered. "I'd only upset the numbers and offend Lady Haggard by not dancing."

Gussie and Marianne Orville were giggling together on the sofa now. Hope, with Susan Laughton, was eyeing them speculatively.

"Why did you invite Hope?" Piers asked suddenly. "He isn't a friend of yours, is he?"

"No. Never met him before the weekend. Irene knew him before." He lowered his head and his voice. "I think she intended him to—er...cheer Jane Bramley up, but she is not interested."

That, at least, cheered Piers.

Excusing himself to the company, he left the drawing room, looking forward to his bed. Before he went upstairs, however, he stuck his head into the library, just in case April awaited him there. He was glad to see she did not, since she could easily be cornered there by the lusty and amoral Hope. He waited five minutes, tapping his fingers on the chess board which still lay there, with the remains of his earlier game.

He hoped Orville would keep his word.

Undisturbed by any other visitor, Piers left the library and climbed the stairs to his bedchamber. As he pushed open the door, he became aware of a graceful figure flitting along the passage toward him.

Recognising her without difficulty, he paused and bowed. "Good night, Mrs. Bramley."

She dropped a demure, half-mocking curtsey. "My lord. It is indeed. You are retiring so early?"

Gazing down at her face—which really was rather lovely in all its understated beauty and curiously warm expression—he no longer felt tired at all.

"It seemed a good idea at the time," he murmured.

"And to me," she said. "It has been a strange few days. In fact, it has been a strange party altogether. You could offer me a nightcap, since I'm sure Irene has left a decanter in your room."

Her meaning was unmistakable, and yet she was not used to seduction. The flush in her pale face, the trembling of her body, told him so. Loneliness washed over him like a tide, along with gratitude and admiration for her courage. Since her face was turned up to his, he took her loosely in his arms and kissed her.

APRIL SAT AT THE KITCHEN table with Cook, Deal, Tilly the maid, and the first footman who was called Leonard. Although she wasn't paying any attention to the conversation, she smiled frequently as she held her tea with both hands and occasionally hummed to herself.

She was looking forward to going to Sillitrees. She had loved being in the country before, when his lordship had taken her to Haybury Court—once she had got used to the vast open spaces, and the silence, and the lack of people. Of course, it wasn't really silent, just that the noises seemed different. She didn't mind that there would be a whole new lot of servants and so-called superiors to get around at Sillitrees. She would still get her reading and writing lessons, and with any luck, Lord Petteril would continue teaching her to ride. She'd always loved horses. And the house would probably be in a state and she could help him decide what to do with it all...

"Got any tea left, Mrs. Varley?" William asked cheerfully, clattering into the kitchen and throwing himself into the vacant chair beside April.

"Drink it quick," Mrs. Varley said, pouring him out a cup. "Time you were in bed since you've an early start in the morning. Nick went up half an hour ago."

"I'll cope. Thanks, Mrs. V." He took the tea, gulped half of it and grinned at April. "Good news that you're staying."

"We're not," April said. "We're leaving tomorrow."

"His lordship is. You're staying here to learn to be her ladyship's new secretary."

Mrs. Varley and Tilly exchanged glances of surprise and some outrage that a stranger should be promoted to such an exalted position.

"No, I ain't," April said. "William's got it wrong."

"Have not," said William, clearly incensed.

"Well, I don't know who told you such nonsense," April began. "But—"

"Lord Petteril himself," William interrupted.

"He wouldn't talk to you about stuff like that," April said scornfully.

"He weren't talking to me," William retorted. "He were talking to the frog, the artist, when I went to light the lamps in the hall. They said as how his lordship was going tomorrow, and you were staying here and how that was best for everyone."

"Rubbish," April said, but it was mechanical, toneless as thoughts swirled in her head with increasing fear. She didn't believe a word of it. William was just larking around, not realizing how upset she'd be... Only William liked her for some reason. He wanted her to stay and he did sound pretty damned pleased with himself.

But Petteril wouldn't discuss her with other people, let alone an artist he barely knew. He'd told her himself that he wouldn't leave her here unless she wished it and he knew she did not. Had someone told him she'd changed her mind? Or had William misunderstood the whole conversation?

A bell jangled above the door.

"Drawing room," Leonard said, getting to his feet. "Come on Tilly, time to clear up the tea things."

"Hope they're not having a late night," Deal said, "'cause they'll be even later tomorrow."

April stared into her tea.

William nudged her elbow. "Ain't that bad here, you know. You'll have respect, good position, friends."

"I got all these already," she retorted. Or had she been fooling herself? She'd always known gentlemen didn't respect people like her, and *he* knew the worst. Was he really determined to decide what was best for her? Or had he had enough of the difficulties caused by keeping her with him? She had always defended him when people jumped to the wrong conclusion, but had she ever truly thought how such mistaken assumptions affected him? She had always been so focused on making sure she stayed because somehow the alternative was unthinkable.

They were friends...

Only, the viscount and the thief from the gutter could never be friends. He had known that as soon as he got his head back together. He had tried to send her away last month after they got Captain Jace, only she'd got round him. Just not for long...maybe.

Leonard returned with an over-burdened tray, Tilly following with cloths and napkins and a small pile of plates.

"They about done up there?" Mrs. Varley asked, rising to her feet.

"The frog's still painting and most of the others are in the drawing room," Leonard reported. He glanced at April. "Your lord's gone to bed. Early start for him, apparently."

That was when she really feared it was true. He would rise at dawn as he always did, and he could leave before she got up and tried to talk him out of it as she always had before.

He was leaving her here so they would both be safe.

Her world, so wonderful only minutes ago, threatened to tumble around her ears. Without *him*, it was cold and lonely and desolate.

She jumped to her feet. *Sod that for a game of soldiers. I got better things to do.*

She meant to go straight up to the attic room she shared with Deal. But nothing in her life had ever been so important as this. She slipped through the door to the second floor, her heart hammering.

If she was caught, she would say she was helping Deal by taking fresh towels to her ladyship's room. Or something. She knew which door that was because Deal had told her. And she knew which door was his lordship's because she'd spent a lot of time getting information casually from the servants as to where everyone slept. It had seemed important when they had been looking for whoever damaged the portrait.

She crept by her ladyship's door and turned the corner.

And then she understood.

Lord Petteril and Mrs. Bramley stood outside his bedchamber door, their arms entwined around each other in a close embrace.

Instantly, April whisked herself away from the unbearable sight, rushing back the way she had come, her breath panting in huge, ragged gasps. *Now* her world had truly crumbled, for now, at last, she understood.

No wife and no mistress would tolerate April in the house. Whichever Mrs. Bramley turned out to be, that was what weighed the scales against her in the end.

CLAUDE ST. ETIENNE had lost track of time. His world had shrunk to his painting, and yet through his art, the world had widened to encompass the truth of man. Somehow it was all embodied in this likeness of an ordinary, likeable man, encompassing all men striving to be good, to be better, as he, St. Etienne, had striven all his life.

Peter Haggard and he were brothers under the skin. All men were brothers. *Liberté, égalité, fraternité,* just as the revolutionaries had preached—before they had turned on him, too. But everyone strived in their own way and they too would find the truth. He forgave them. He forgave everyone.

St. Etienne knew he was exhausted, but the blood still rushed through his veins as he finally stood back and saw his vision. This was a great portrait. He, Claude St. Etienne was a great artist at last, producing a unique work, full of truth and beauty and stark reality.

With pride, he scrawled his name at the bottom in white paint. Only then did he drop the brush. He should clean his brushes, tidy...

A slight movement caught his attention and he turned with delight. "You! Now my world is perfect. Rejoice with me."

And then the whole world was pain.

IT WAS STILL DARK WHEN Piers woke. He did not know what had disturbed him, for he still felt tired enough to have slept for another hour. His heart was beating too fast, as though after a nasty dream, probably the falling one, although he couldn't remember. Unease filled him. Something was wrong.

He sat up and lit the lamp. Still groggy with sleep, he dredged up the events of the previous evening. Orville. St. Etienne and his portrait. And today he was leaving Pelton Park for Sillitrees. He would be glad to go. But first, he needed to speak to April. Then he would know...

His mind wandered back to his reasonless unease. His stomach felt tight and knotted. He threw off the blankets and padded over to the washstand. Washing in cold water certainly dealt with the cloying tendrils of sleep. Hastily, he climbed into his riding clothes as usual. He would have a quick gallop on Haggard's amiable horse and have breakfast before he sent for April and took his leave of Haggs and Lady Haggs. With or without her.

When he blew out the lamp, the very first slivers of pre-dawn grey showed beyond the window, though it was probably too dark just yet to ride safely without a lantern. Silently, taking his candle, he left his room and made his way along the passage to the staircase.

None of the servants were up yet. He decided to use the side door, since it was quieter to unlock, but at the foot of the stair he paused.

The door to St. Etienne's studio was ajar and swaying slightly as though in a gentle draught. Had St. Etienne left the window open to release the paint fumes?

With odd reluctance, he forced his feet to walk, one after the other, and pushed open the door to the studio.

One of the windows was wide open, stirring the curtain. The room was cold and gloomy. Lighting the nearest lamp, Piers held it high and turned back to face the room.

On the wooden armchair sat St. Etienne himself, apparently asleep. Except a gilt picture frame was wrapped around his neck like a scarf. The wooden backing and a painted canvas stuck up behind his head.

Piers did not speak. He knew as he walked over that the man was dead. Still, he went through the motions, looking for a pulse, a breath. There was none. He felt cold to the touch.

And then he saw that the painting which had been broken over the dead man's head was the partially repaired portrait of Sir Weston Haggard.

BEFORE BOLTING UPSTAIRS to wake Haggs, Piers took the key from the inside of the "studio" door and locked it from the outside. Then he dashed across the hall and pushed open the green baize door to the servants' quarters.

There was no noise yet, no chatter or banging of pots and pans. But it would not be long before the first servants were up and about their duties. Since he was there already, he used the back stairs to get to the second floor. He knew Haggs still resided in the same rooms he had had as a boy. Out of respect to his stepmother, he had never moved into his father's rooms.

He did not really expect Haggs to wake up and hear his faint scratch at the door, which was purely perfunctory for he opened it almost at once and went in. Crossing the cluttered sitting room to the half-open bedchamber door, he stuck his head in.

"Haggs," he said low and urgently, "you have to wake up."

"No, I don't," Haggs mumbled. "Master of my own house. Bugger off, Withy." Then after a short silence. "Withy?" The tousled head reared off the pillow, peering toward Piers's candle.

"St. Etienne's dead," Piers said. "I'm sorry. Someone broke your father's portrait over his head. Which room is Orville's?"

"*Orville's?*" Haggs scrubbed his hands over his face and hair as though trying to establish he was awake and not dreaming. "Next on the left."

"You have to get up and send for the doctor and the magistrate," Piers said, not without sympathy. "And you must look after your stepmother. I've locked the studio door."

"Is that where he is?"

Piers nodded, which his friend probably could not even see in the gloom, but he was already on his way out.

He did not knock on Orville's door, simply opened it and went in. The shutters were not closed, nor the curtains on either the window or the bed, so the pale glimmerings of early dawn had seeped in. For a second, he gazed at the still, huddled figure in the bed, listening to the deep, even breathing. If the man was not asleep, he was very good at pretending.

Piers glanced around, saw the gleam of a white letter propped up on the dressing table. Piers raised his candle and saw it was sealed and directed to Lady Haggard. Another behind it was addressed to Sir Peter Haggard.

It looked as if Orville intended to do exactly as he had said—leave Pelton Park with a full confession and apology to his hosts for what he had done. But defacing a painting that did not belong to you was a moment of madness, an act of vandalism, a petty crime of annoyance and bad taste. Killing a man was entirely different.

Had Orville's temper struck again?

Piers could not imagine him going so far. He doubted he had it in him. And yet...he had been wrong already. He had been so sure he understood the motive behind the vandalism. So unforgivably sure, as it turned out, because St. Etienne was dead. Never in his wildest speculations had he foreseen this tragedy.

He left the room and encountered Haggs in the passage.

"Show me," Haggs said grimly.

"SOMEONE MUST HAVE COME in the window to rob us," Haggs said, five minutes later. "And panicked to see the room occupied."

"And hit him with your father's portrait because it was the nearest weapon to hand?" Piers said. "It's a damned unfortunate painting."

"What do you think happened then?"

"I don't know. I need to see more and learn more and think."

"And I need to summon the magistrate," Haggs muttered, striding toward the bell pull. At the easel, he paused, staring. They had lit all the lamps and the new portrait glistened and gleamed. "Damn. Is that really me?"

"Good, isn't it?" Piers managed. "He was proud of it and rightly so."

Haggs went into the hall to meet whoever answered his ring and issue his orders. Piers walked slowly about the room, remembering it as it had been yesterday evening when he had last seen St. Etienne.

The palette lay on the table beside the chest, the little splodges of paint mostly used and drying. Everything else was neatly away, the brushes cleaned and ready. Piers looked again at Haggs's portrait, which was finished and signed. The man must have worked half the night.

And then what? Fallen asleep in the chair, where he was attacked by a stranger climbing in the window? By Orville, deciding that defacing the artist's portraits was not punishment enough? By someone else Piers had not even considered?

Piers walked to the window. It had been closed when he had looked in yesterday evening, the paint fumes strong but not overwhelming. The room was large and airy. Now the window sash was up as far as it would go. Piers stuck his head out. A man could easily climb in from the ground and climb out again with his bag of swag.

A memory hit him of the small thief in his London house, a few bits of linen, silk and cuff links stuffed into a calico bag. Hazy and yet imprinted on his mind because of what had come after.

As he started to withdraw his head, a movement in the distance caught his attention. Clear in the growing dawn light, a female in familiar-looking maid's cap and woollen cloak was driving a gig down the lesser drive used by servants and tradesmen. Groping for his quizzing glass, Piers focused more closely. It *was* April.

Where the devil is she going at this hour?

Wherever, it certainly wasn't making her happy. Her shoulders, her whole body seemed to droop as she drove out of his sight. She hadn't looked back, only straight ahead. Something was wrong. Wrong enough to tug hard at his already knotted stomach.

Had someone hurt her? Had that bastard Hope laid a finger on her?

Terrified for her well-being, he bolted into the hall, almost falling over Haggs who, having instructed his servants, was trying to come back into the room.

"What...?" Haggs gasped.

"Back soon!" Piers threw over his shoulder. Leaping over the maid who was beginning to polish the brasses on the open front door, he flew down the steps and round to the stables.

Chapter Ten

In time, April would wish him well. She wanted him to be happy and she understood only too well his terrible loneliness. She had feared Louise Austen for that reason, afraid he would marry her without love just because she was more interesting than most.

Jane Bramley must be, too. She was likeable, apparently, and virtuous, and she already had the experience of marriage.

April didn't want to think about that.

Having harnessed the pony herself and put it between the shafts of the gig, she told the yawning groom who wandered into the yard that he could pick them up from the village inn later on. Then she climbed up, gathered the reins, and set off for her new life.

There was no joy in it, no excitement. In time, she would have to think of practicalities, how to survive on her own, though she didn't doubt that she could. She had done it all her life. It didn't make her proud as she drove down the track and veered out the small, open gate into the road. She turned right toward the village and lost herself in the kind of misery that blocked all sensible thought.

An old lady walked past her in the opposite direction, carrying a bundle of wood. April nodded curtly in response to her greeting. She didn't even glance at the young farm labourers who tried to stop and chat, just let the pony shove them out of the way.

She shook the reins impatiently. "Can't you go any faster?"

The pony broke into a reluctant trot, which was a good thing. She wanted to be well away before Petteril started for Sillitrees. Her heart tightened and she urged the pony faster.

The thundering hooves seemed to come out of nowhere. In reality, they must have been audible for some time, but April didn't notice until they were almost upon her. In sudden alarm, she whipped her head around. A hatless horseman was racing beside her.

He looked alarmingly like Petteril, except there was no vagueness or humour in the determined face. And there was no saddle on the horse, she saw in amazement as he drew abreast of her, and no stirrups, only a bridle.

Before she realized what he was about, he streaked further ahead and, reaching over, caught the pony's head and brought him to a stand-still. Jesus, it *was* Petteril.

"Oi!" she said indignantly.

"Where the devil do you think you're going?"

"None of your business," she retorted. "I've given notice."

He blinked. "To whom?"

"William," she said defiantly. "He's putting it in your room."

There was confusion in his eyes, reminding her of the first time she had seen him, except they were not dull, but angry, which was rare enough to claw at her stomach.

"Why?" he asked baffled. "If you want to stay at Pelton, you could just have told me."

"I ain't staying at Pelton," she said with unnecessary aggression. "It's boring."

He blinked. "Is it? St. Etienne is dead."

That broke through her furious misery. Her jaw probably dropped as she stared at him. "Dead? How?"

"Someone broke Sir Weston's portrait over his head."

She closed her mouth and swallowed until hysteria subsided and he held her gaze with unusual sternness.

"I need your help," he said.

Her stupid heart leapt before reality broke in. "No, you don't, mister. It's you who solves the mysteries. I just do what you tell me."

"Not very often." Still holding the pony's bridle, he began to lead it around to face the other way.

"I ain't going back to Pelton!" she said in panic. "I won't stay there."

"Don't then," he said, tugging the pony sharply to avoid the ditch at the side of the road. Once the pony and the gig were straight, he released the bridle and clicked his tongue to get the animal to walk on. He no longer looked at her. "Did someone hurt you?"

Only you, mister, only you... She shook her head, unable to see for the sudden tears and furiously blinking them away.

"Then what the devil got into you? Why were you going to leave the pony and gig at the inn?"

"'Cause I'm leaving on my terms, not yours."

Although she didn't look at him, she knew from his voice exactly the perplexed frown tugging at his brow. "Two days ago, you were sulking because you thought—without any evidence—that I was going to drop you on Lady Haggard. Now you're bolting because I'm not?"

"Because you *are*!" she hurled at him. "William heard you say so."

He was about to retort when, through her furious blinking, she saw his expression change to one of thoughtfulness. "Was that your William skulking in the hall outside the studio last evening?"

"He ain't my William!"

"Maybe he should be. I don't know which of you is dafter. St. Etienne said something about you staying on with Lady Haggard. She must have mentioned the possibility to him days ago, or he overheard servants' gossip. I certainly never said anything of the kind. I always said I would speak to you first. We owe each other that."

The heat of shame flamed up over her face.

"Why didn't you ask me?" he asked more gently.

"I meant to," she mumbled. "You were busy." She drew in her breath and said in a rush, "I know no lady'll put up with me in your house, but I won't wait to be driven out."

Only pride allowed her to glare straight into his eyes. Rather to her surprise, a tinge of colour crept along his lean cheekbones. He knew she had seen him with Mrs. Bramley.

"I'm the viscount," he said sternly. "No one else drives my people and I'm more likely to beat them than dismiss them."

A sob rose up her throat. She pretended it was laughter. "No, you're not."

"I'll make an exception in your case if you ever take off like that again without a word."

Shock still had her in its grip, so it was a while before she caught up with the change in her reality.

He rode beside her on Sir Peter's horse, tall, long-legged, controlling the animal easily with one hand, as if keeping the other free to grab the pony if she bolted again.

"Where d'you learn to ride without a saddle, then?" she demanded.

"Boy's trick," he said vaguely. His thoughts clearly were somewhere else. With the dead man, perhaps, or still with her...

Wonder spread through her slowly. "You came and got me," she blurted.

"I'll always come and get you."

And that, April thought, was pure happiness.

PIERS'S NERVES STILL jangled with relief that she was not harmed, that he had caught her before she disappeared alone into some unknown world of danger. Like the one he'd plucked her from more by accident than design. He felt sick because she did not trust him, because she had never had any reason to trust anyone.

They stood side by side in the studio, gazing down at the dead figure of poor Claude St. Etienne. Sir Peter, apparently, was with his stepmother.

"Poor devil," April breathed. "They must have hit him with some force. You been through his clothes?"

"Not yet. I was distracted. You look." Piers was looking at the head wound. Gingerly, he fingered through the curls.

The backing of the portrait had been quite flimsy though the frame itself was heavy. It had made a sickening dent in St. Etienne's skull.

"There's not much blood," Piers said thoughtfully, "considering how hard he must have been hit."

"What does that mean?"

"I suppose, that he died quickly. Which is something. Anything in his pockets?"

April straightened with a penknife in one hand and a screwed up paper in the other. She opened the folded knife and found it clean, apart from a few specks of paint, none of them the colour of blood. She sniffed the twisted paper and wrinkled her nose.

"I've smelled that somewhere before," she said.

Piers took it from her and drew back in distaste. "So have I. Opium. I saw him put a powder in his wine at dinner once. He suffered from migraines."

A knock sounded on the studio door.

"Enter," Piers said distractedly.

Yates appeared in the doorway. "Mr. Quarles and Dr. Robertson have arrived, my lord. Shall I show them straight in here?"

Quarles was the local magistrate.

"Yes, please, Yates," Piers said, "and you'd better inform Sir Peter."

"Of course, my lord." Yates bowed the gentlemen in and departed.

Mr. Quarles, a bustling man of middle years and stocky stature, strode into the room and halted so suddenly that the taller, younger man behind almost cannoned into him.

"What are you doing to the body?" Quarles demanded. "Who the devil are you? Girl, away with you!"

April stepped back, more to get out of Piers's way, he suspected, than to obey the newcomer in any way.

Piers went forward to greet them, hand outstretched. "I'm Petteril."

The bustling Quarles's eyebrows flew up. "Lord Petteril? Why, so you are! We met several years ago at Pelton Park. How do you do, my lord? This is Dr. Robertson." Before Piers could shake hands with the doctor too, the magistrate was striding toward the body saying, "Bad business, bad business... Good God, what happened?"

"That is how I found him," Piers said.

"Must have been dashed early," Quarles said, staring at poor St. Etienne.

"I suffer from insomnia. I was going to walk until it was light enough to ride. But in the hall, I felt the draught and came in to see that all was well. St. Etienne was hard at work yesterday evening. When I found him this morning, he was like that."

"And the window was open? Some lunatic, a burglar maybe, clearly climbed in and did that to him. What is the world coming to? A gentleman isn't safe in his own home. Who is the poor fellow again?"

As the doctor edged past and began to examine the body, Petteril replied, "Claude St. Etienne. Émigré portrait painter, commissioned by Lady Haggard to paint Sir Peter, I believe, and clean up a few older paintings. But Haggard will give you the details of that."

The doctor, after a good look, was lifting the broken painting off the body. April sprang forward to help as one of the thin backing strips of wood was about to fall. Setting all the bits on the floor, he turned back to St. Etienne, inspecting his scalp much as Petteril had done earlier. Then he lifted the eyelids, pulled down the loose cravat from his neck and pulled up the smock.

"Help me?" he said to no one in particular, pulling the torso toward himself. Piers steadied the chair and, like the doctor, peered at the back of the body.

"What are you looking for, doctor?" he asked.

"Other injury," the doctor said, laying the body back again. "I wouldn't have expected the picture to cause quite such catastrophic damage. Either it killed him outright or..."

"Or what?" Quarles demanded impatiently.

"Or he was already dead when he was hit."

Quarles stared at him. "Why would anyone hit a dead man?"

"I don't know that anyone did," Dr. Robertson said patiently. "I need to examine the body properly to establish how he died. May I take him now?"

Quarles, scowling, waved one hand in permission and the doctor strode to the door, summoning his henchmen. At that point Haggs appeared, pale and harassed looking.

"Thanks for coming so promptly," he said.

"Terrible business," Quarles said. "It must be a great shock for poor Lady Haggard."

"She is in pieces," Haggs said, shaking his head violently as though angry with the whole, incomprehensible world. "Somehow, it makes it all so much worse because it was done with my father's portrait."

"Oh, dear Lord," Quarles exclaimed, staring at the pieces on the floor. "I didn't even notice that! What a vile thing..."

Haggs met Piers's gaze in unspoken question, clearly wondering whether or not to tell the magistrate about the portrait's earlier defacement. Piers, who didn't know whether his friend was aware that his cousin had confessed to that crime, shook his head infinitesimally. There would be time enough to explain all to the magistrate if necessary.

"I'm afraid all this must have rather spoiled your party plans," Quarles said as he prepared to depart. "My sympathy and regards to her ladyship. Mrs. Quarles and I were looking forward to coming this evening, but of course, it will no longer happen."

"Sadly not," Haggs said bleakly, walking with them to the front door.

Temporarily alone with April, to whom no one had paid any attention, Piers stared at the broken portrait. "Was I wrong in the first place? Did Orville deceive me somehow, covering for someone else?"

"It fits him," April said.

"I thought it suited Mrs. Laughton too. Did I just *make* it fit Orville?" *Did my mistake cause St. Etienne's death*?

April was silent, for which he was grateful.

Pulling himself together, he began to walk away. "I need to change. I smell of horse."

Her head jerked up in alarm. "Wait, mister, my letter's still up there. Don't read it, just burn it."

"That bad?" he said ruefully.

Her skin was flushed, her dark blue eyes intense. "Promise me you'll burn it."

He sighed. "I promise."

But when he got to his room, he saw the letter at once, propped up on the mantelpiece with *Lord Petteril* written neatly across the front. He picked it up to admire the improvement in her letters. A small stain marred the corner, as though she had spilled a drop of moisture on it. Or a tear. His stomach twisted.

He did not have time even to think about this, let alone decide what to do. So he put the letter back on the mantelpiece and changed into correct morning dress.

INEVITABLY, THE NEWS that the Frenchman was dead had spread around the entire household before breakfast. Details, including the role of Sir Weston's portrait, were kept from everyone else, except Yates, the close-lipped butler.

Susan Laughton, told of the sudden death by her maid, was devastated and sobbed in her husband's arms.

Pathetically glad that she needed him for something, Matthew Laughton held her, his cheek to her hair, girding himself up to be pitied once more as the husband taking second place not only to the late Sir Weston Haggard, but to the late third rate painter.

Was it worth it, to see the back of the little snake?

"There, there," he crooned to his wife. "You must not let the world see how much you care."

She let out a gasp and pulled free. "Oh no, how could I be so selfish? Poor Irene! Poor, poor Irene! I must go to her..."

And Susan fled from the room, leaving Laughton scratching his head. Irene Haggard, too? What did all these women see in the French runt?

Oh well, at least he was dead.

An instant of shame crept up on him, quickly squashed.

Laughton finished tying his cravat and, hearing voices outside, glanced out of the window.

A cart was being loaded with a human-shaped bundle wrapped in blankets. Two rough looking men covered him in a tarpaulin, which they tied to the side of the cart, before jumping up into the seat and setting off.

The cart followed the magistrate's carriage toward the drive.

The sight of the covered body was curiously upsetting, almost like grief. Laughton had not liked St. Etienne, but there was something tragic in a vital, living being reduced so quickly to that still bundle of nothing loaded onto a cart.

Laughton shivered, wondering if anyone knew how he had died.

He thought, briefly, of waiting for Susan to return, but she was just as likely to go down to breakfast with Irene or anyone else. So, with one last glance at his reflection in the mirror—really, he was not an illfavoured fellow—he set off downstairs to the breakfast parlour.

Here, he found Lady Petteril and her daughter, Mrs. Bramley, and, more surprisingly, Randal Hope.

"At this hour, Hope?" Laughton murmured, standing next to him as they both helped themselves from the dishes arrayed upon the sideboard.

"Astonishing, isn't it? There was just so much racket going on, inside the house and out, that I couldn't get off to sleep again. I thought I might as well eat." He headed back to the table, calling over his shoulder, "I suppose you've heard the news? The dashed frog is dead."

A twitch of distaste curled at Mrs. Bramley's lips. Lady Petteril looked both shocked and disapproving. But only little Miss Withan chose to tell him off.

"You need not sound so pleased about it. The magistrate might well look at you for the crime."

"What crime?" Hope returned. "The fellow's portrait was the crime if you ask me."

"Didn't you hear?" Laughton said, deciding on two eggs rather than just the one. "The magistrate and the doctor were here. The coroner too, for all I know. I wonder if someone hit him too hard?"

"Mr. Laughton!" Lady Petteril exclaimed, lunging toward her daughter as though she would cover the girl's ears.

"The magistrate might *well* be looking at you, then," Hope said nastily to Laughton.

"Or you," Laughton retorted. "After all, you made no secret of the fact you despised him."

"I did." Hope sat down beside Gussie Withan. "Not worth my effort to let *his* claret."

"A little respect, sir, if you please," Mrs. Bramley said quietly. "We are not all as comfortable with sudden death as you appear to be."

Laughton pretended not to hear her. "It was probably whoever defaced Sir Weston's portrait," he said, moving to the table.

Kenneth Orville, who had just come in, looked as if he was about to bolt back out, except that Mrs. Bramley called at once, "Any news, Mr. Orville?"

Orville shook his head. "Monsieur St. Etienne is definitely deceased. I believe the magistrate has been and gone. Mrs. Laughton is with Lady Haggard. But I beg you will not discuss it further in front of my sister."

White-faced and yet avid, Miss Orville entered behind her brother and rushed over to sit opposite Gussie.

It was going to be a long and tedious day.

Chapter Eleven

"**I**s it related to the original vandalism?" Haggs asked Piers. They were standing together, gazing at St. Etienne's magnificent portrait of the former.

"I think it must be. I thought I knew who the vandal was but now..."

"Who?" Haggs asked, frowning.

Piers exhaled slowly. "I think I need to speak to you and Lady Haggard together. Will she see us?"

Haggs nodded. "Yes. But this has hit her hard, Withy. I think it brings back my father's death and that makes everything worse."

Piers made no reply, merely jerked his head at April, who followed them in silence. No one told her off for not using the servants' stairs.

Deal opened the door, but Piers could hear at once that another woman was present too. It was Susan Laughton's distinctive, smooth yet throaty voice, wobbling now in grief.

"She needs to go, sir," Deal murmured to Haggs.

"I'll see to it," Haggs said grimly.

In the sitting room, Lady Haggard was wearing only a voluminous robe. Her eyes were heavy, her face white, her lips stiff with the effort of exerting patience.

"Forgive the interruption," Haggs said. "I'm sorry, Mrs. Laughton, but I need to speak to my stepmother alone."

"Of course." Mrs. Laughton rose, the picture of tragedy, and glided toward the door, where she waited an instant, as though expecting Piers to follow her.

April stood very still, blending into the background as Mrs. Laughton left. Deal jerked her head but April, apparently, did not see.

"Do you mind if April stays?" Piers asked Lady Haggard. "She is very useful at taking notes."

"Notes of what?" Lady Haggard asked in a bewildered voice, as April sat down by the desk and took out her notebook and pencil.

"I am afraid I need to ask you more questions, in the light of Monsieur St. Etienne's death."

"It is the magistrate's business now," Lady Haggard said. "Your service to us is discharged."

"Is it?" At her ladyship's invitation, Piers sat in the chair opposite her. Haggs meandered to the window. "Have you seen Mr. Orville this morning?"

"Kenneth? No, why...? Oh, Deal sent him away but he left a letter of some kind. It's on the desk beside you, April."

April turned, found the only letter on top of the desk, and took it to Lady Haggard, who broke the seal, frowning.

Haggs gazed enquiringly at Piers, who deliberately kept his attention on Lady Haggard's face. It was up to her how much she told her stepson about Orville's motives for what he had done. Or said he had done.

Her eyes widened and she gave a little gasp. Her lips whitened. He could not see her eyes.

"Irene?" Haggs said quickly, but when she raised her eyes, it was to look directly at Piers.

Behind her grief was a spark of genuine anger. "Is this true?"

"I don't know," Piers replied. "I believed it yesterday, which is why I told you Mrs. Laughton was innocent. I presume Orville writes what he told me he would."

Irene's gaze moved to Haggs. "He writes that he defaced your father's portrait, in a moment of madness and anger at me. He 'blinded' the portrait so that your father would not 'see' what I had become."

"And what have you become?" Haggs asked with a scowl of outrage clearly directed at his cousin, not his stepmother.

She shrugged. "A little lonely. A little foolish." Her chin tilted. "I took a lover. I'm sorry."

Haggard's breath might have caught. His eyelids definitely swept down to hide whatever emotion he was feeling, but when he lifted them again, there was no sign of anger, only rueful understanding.

"Don't apologise to me. My father has been dead for more than two years. Does it hurt very much that St. Etienne is gone too?"

A single sob racked her. "You know!"

"I guessed," he said gently. "I don't grudge you and it's certainly not Kenneth's place to do so. On the other hand," he said, striding over to Piers, "you surely don't think Kenneth Orville *murdered* St. Etienne?"

"I don't know," Piers said. "I had it in my head that the vandalism was not about St. Etienne at all, but about Sir Weston and the powerful feelings of love and loyalty he inspired in people. But what if I am wrong? What if it was always about St. Etienne? Who hated him enough to spoil his work and kill him with his own painting?"

"According to the quack," April's voice said from the back of the room, where she had once again retreated to the desk, "it weren't necessarily the painting what killed him."

Lady Haggard stared at her as though she had forgotten her presence, if not her existence. "What else could it be?"

"There was no other obvious injury," Piers said. "But the doctor will perform an autopsy to try and discover the precise cause of death."

"One would think the cause of death obvious to the meanest of intelligence," Haggs said, scowling. "Not sure I care for Dr. Robertson after all. Let the poor bas—man—rest in peace."

"He looked quite peaceful," April assured him. "His eyes were closed."

Piers blinked and turned his head to gaze at her.

She stared at him almost defiantly. "All the dead folk I've seen just after, their eyes are open."

"Have you seen many?" Lady Haggard asked, a little tartly.

"Loads. Violent and natural."

Lady Haggard's expression altered to one of appalled pity. April seemed to be regarding her in much the same way. On the meaner back streets of London, rife with crime and poverty, violent death was not rare. April had grown up with its constant presence. While St. Etienne was her ladyship's first encounter.

"Did you see St. Etienne after dinner yesterday?" Piers asked Lady Haggard.

"Not until I was about to retire. About eleven of the clock. He was hard at work on Peter's portrait so I left him to it."

Piers glanced at Haggs. "And you? Did you sit for him in the evening?"

"No, he seemed to be painting from memory and a few earlier sketches he had done."

Piers looked from him to his stepmother and back. "Is that normal for him?"

"Yes, I think so," Lady Haggard said. "I think Weston only sat for him once or twice, quite briefly."

"Did he paint Sir Weston in a day, too?"

"No," Lady Haggard said thoughtfully. "Over several days. He even asked him to sit once more and made some corrections with the light and shadow."

"Then he was in a hurry doing Peter's... Why would that be? Was he planning to leave Pelton Park?"

"Not for another week."

"Perhaps he just wanted to get it out of the way so he could relax and enjoy himself," Haggs said.

His stepmother flushed but did not dispute it.

Piers said, "Was the window open when you looked in on him last night?"

She frowned. "Actually, yes it was."

Piers shifted uncomfortably in his chair. "Forgive me, but when did your *affaire* with St. Etienne begin?"

"Only a little more than a week ago. A couple of days after he arrived. He said he wanted to paint me instead of Peter, that he had always wanted to paint me. I told him Peter was his commission, but I was touched." She raised one shaking hand to wipe away the tear at the corner of her eye. "I thought there would be time. Later."

She turned to Piers, a smile trembling on her lips. "He wanted to paint you too when you arrived. He didn't seem particularly eager to paint Peter, and yet his portrait of him is surely a masterpiece."

"It is," Piers agreed, remembering the brush flying across the canvas, bold and quick, the artist's whole being totally focused, his talent flowing out of him and into the painting as though nothing and no one could stop him. He glanced at Haggs. "I don't suppose you saw him after eleven?"

Haggs shook his head. "No, I went straight up to bed—I think everyone did—about half past eleven."

Piers tapped one finger against his upper lip, and focused his attention back to Lady Haggard. "Why did he take opium?"

"For the headaches, which were quite severe."

"How long had he suffered with migraines?" Piers asked, dropping his hand into his lap. "How often did he get them?"

"I think he always had them. And I don't really know. He hid them from people, tried to work through them if he could. Why do you ask?"

"I don't know," Piers admitted. "I suppose I can't help thinking I should have paid more attention to St. Etienne in the first place. Did Orville like him?"

"Not really," Haggs replied. "Didn't like a Frenchman being in the house, but Kenneth is not violent, Piers."

"He has a temper, though." Piers glimpsed the further unease in Haggard's eyes and rose quickly to his feet. "Sorry. I am thinking aloud. I don't honestly think he is a murderer—apart from anything else, why write a letter of apology to Lady Haggard for defacing her painting, and then trot downstairs and deface the artist as well?"

"With the same painting," April pointed out, scribbling something in her book.

"Exactly. Whatever happened, we need evidence, proof. Apart from you and the Laughtons, did anyone else in the house know him before he arrived at Pelton Park two weeks ago?"

"Not that I know of," Lady Haggard said.

"May I search his bedchamber?"

"And his things in the studio if you think they'll help," Lady Haggard said. "But doesn't it seem to you more likely that...?"

"That what, my lady?"

"That someone simply entered the house through the open window, attacked him and then fled?"

Piers had already thought about it. "No. It doesn't seem likely at all. Though it cannot be ruled out. I'd like to go and speak to your other guests, if I may."

"I'll come with you," Haggs said. "Lend you my support."

"What of you, April?" Lady Haggard said unexpectedly.

"She missed breakfast," Piers said sternly. "I'm sending her to the kitchen to eat some, and then she can help me search through St. Etienne's things."

It was a moot point, Piers reflected, when he and Haggs found the other guests gathered in the breakfast parlour, whether he questioned them more than they questioned him. Eager for news of what had really happened to St. Etienne, they seemed to him like ghouls or vultures. His aunt made it plain she would answer no questions on her movements from her impertinent nephew and Gussie assured him they had retired early, before eleven and they had not seen poor Monsieur St. Etienne since dinner last night.

Apart from Matthew Laughton, who said suddenly, "Wait, though, I did go to his studio quite late. After everyone had retired, I suddenly remembered I'd been going to ask his availability to paint my brother's family—I thought I would make it a Christmas gift. So I went to see if he was still in his studio."

"And was he?" Piers said, sparing a quick glance at Susan Laughton before returning to her husband.

"Yes, painting feverishly and refusing to discuss anything further until his portrait of Haggard was finished. And actually," Laughton added, taking out his snuff box and helping himself to a pinch, "it did look very good—unless he spoiled it later."

"He did not," Piers assured him. "What did you do then? How long did you stay in the studio with him?"

"About half a minute. He was clearly opposed to company."

"What time was this, sir?" Piers asked.

Laughton glanced at his wife. "About half past eleven, I think."

"Was the window in the studio open?"

Laughton blinked. This time he did not look at his wife. "No."

"Are you sure?"

"Of course," Laughton said haughtily. "You have reason to doubt me, my lord?"

"Actually, yes," Piers said. "The window was closed when I saw him at nine. But it was open when Lady Haggard looked in at eleven. By the time you went in at half past, it was closed again. And yet wide open before five this morning."

"Why should he not open and close the window as often as he chooses?"

"No reason," Piers said. "But if you didn't actually notice the window, I wish you would say so." Orville caught his attention, moving rapidly from the table to the door.

Hastily, Piers bowed to the company, thanked them and, leaving Haggs to the tender mercy of his guests' curiosity, he caught up with Orville in the hall.

"I presented my letter to Lady Haggard this morning," he blurted, "and left one for Peter, too. I meant to depart this morning, to spare them any embarrassment, but now, with St. Etienne's death, I'm not sure I should. Would I be too unwelcome to be any kind of help to either of them?"

"I don't honestly know," Piers said. "Did you speak to St. Etienne last night?"

Orville shook his head violently. "God, no." He stared at Piers with growing despair. "You think I killed him, don't you? Just because I spoiled the portrait!"

"Could you prove that you did not?"

"No," said Orville, "but I know you cannot prove that I did,"

As Orville stalked outside, Piers climbed the stairs and went in search of St. Etienne's bedchamber. He found it easily, in the end, because April was already in there and had left the door open.

She looked up from the chest of drawers she was plundering. "Find out anything?"

"Not really. Except Laughton lied about going to the studio last night."

"How d'you know?" April closed the top drawer with an air of dissatisfaction and looked around her.

"Because he said he was there at half past eleven and the window was closed. Lady Haggard said it was open when she left at eleven. And it seemed to me St. Etienne was far too absorbed in his painting to be constantly opening and closing the window."

"Why would Laughton lie though?" April moved toward the bedside table.

Piers crouched down on the other side of the bed and pulled out a large carpet bag. "Protecting someone who had been there, probably. He just forgot to get all the details from her before he talked."

"He was covering for his wife?" April paused her hand on the first of two drawers in the cabinet.

"Probably." Piers swept his hands around the inside of the empty bag. "St. Etienne rejected her for Irene, much as Sir Weston did years ago. It gives Susan a motive."

"Gives him one an' all," April said, "if his wife fancied St. Etienne. In fact, he's more able to belt the poor man over the head with the picture than she is."

"True. But he's not thinking of that, only of distracting any attention from her."

April wrenched open the drawer. "Why can't people just tell the tru—" She broke off, staring.

Piers stood up and leaned over the bed to see into the drawer. It was stuffed with little folded papers of the kind he had seen St. Etienne empty into his wine. April took one from the drawer and unfolded it before setting it on the bed.

Piers reached over and stuck his finger in the powder. But he knew before he touched his tongue to it. "Opium."

April closed the drawer and opened the one beneath. It, too, was full of the same kind of folded papers.

"That's a lot of opium," she observed.

"He must have had a lot of headaches."

"Or he was selling it to other people," April said.

"He was setting up as an apothecary?"

"People like that stuff. Mind you, it can turn your brain to mush." Becoming aware of his gaze, she lifted her bleak eyes to his. "I seen it. They'll kill for it. Literally."

Shocked out of his own black memories, he blinked. "You think he was killed for *this*? That someone really did climb in the window, murder St. Etienne when he couldn't get any opium out of him, then climb back out again?"

April kicked the open drawer. "Except I don't see why he wouldn't hand it over. He's got enough. But it could have something to do with it. People who smuggle it in ain't kind and caring."

Alarming possibilities reared up in his mind. He stuffed the paper of opium into his pocket. "Keep looking," he said over his shoulder, already half-way to the door.

APRIL BURROWED INSIDE the pillowcases and underneath the mattress. Discovering nothing, she went back to the chest of drawers, running her hands over the inside of the cabinet and beneath each drawer in case something was affixed there. It wasn't.

The desk was even less interesting. He had been at Pelton a fortnight, but no half-written correspondence littered the surface. If he had received any letters, he must have destroyed them.

Two spare coats hung in his wardrobe. She went through the pockets, but he hadn't hidden any private letters there either. He must have been focused entirely on his art. But she began to see him not just as an intensely private man, but a lonely one. Was that what had drawn Lady Haggard to him? She found only a few coins, a full paper of powder, and a screwed up empty one.

"What are you planning to do with that?" drawled a voice from the doorway.

April spun around and beheld Randal Hope, suave and elegant in perfect morning clothes, strolling into the room. With one casual kick, he closed the door behind him.

Chapter Twelve

Deal looked outraged to see Piers back again.

"Is her ladyship here or downstairs?" he enquired politely.

"I am here," Lady Haggard said briskly, as, over Deal's shoulder, he saw her emerge beautifully dressed in grey with a black shawl.

One must mourn to be decent, but it would not have done to overemphasise the degree of mourning. Fleetingly, Piers remembered the time there had been nothing but mourning in his own family. The whole world had been black, scholarship his only release. And then, with the final grief, that had been taken from him, too.

And yet here he stood.

"Come in, my lord. What can I help you with?"

Deal remained by the door like a sentry on watch. Piers did not sit when Lady Haggard did, though he stood by the sofa opposite her.

"My lady, do you happen to know why Monsieur St. Etienne might have taken opium?"

"For his migraines," she replied at once. Sorting through the things in her reticule, she did not even need to think about the answer. "He suffered from them terribly. I told you so earlier."

"You did. Then he took opium regularly?"

"Only if his poor head plagued him. Deal, would you bring me a handkerchief?"

"My lady." The maid bustled away toward the bedchamber.

"Do you keep any in the house?" Piers asked.

Lady Haggard glanced up in surprise. "A small bottle of laudanum in the medicine chest, though it is not much used. It was a Godsend, though, when one of our labourers sliced a finger off with his scythe."

"Recently?" Piers pounced.

"Oh, three years ago. Nearly four."

"Then he does not still take it?"

"Lord no, he's fit as a flea. He doesn't even notice the finger anymore, according to his wife. Why do you ask?"

"I'm interested in who else in the neighbourhood might take opium for whatever reason."

Lady Haggard took the clean wisp of lace from Deal and dropped it into her reticule before closing it. "I can think of no one."

"Not even among your other guests?"

"I believe Susan Laughton took a drop of laudanum for a while to help her sleep, but Matthew did not approve and she stopped."

"To please her husband?" Piers asked in surprise.

"Or herself. Either way, she told me last year she avoided it. None of the others ever mentioned such a thing to me. Oh, except—" She broke off. "No matter. No one mentioned it."

"Please. It is important."

She smiled a little nervously. "Gussie happened to mention that her mother took the occasional drop. It was prescribed to her by her physician after the death of her sons."

"But that was laudanum. Not opium in powder form?"

"Perhaps you should ask her," Lady Haggard said. Despite the gentleness of her voice, it was a challenge. The world knew of the difficult relationship between the new viscount and the dowager, and no doubt few fancied Petteril's chances in a quarrel.

Lady Haggard rose, making clear the interview was at an end.

Obediently, Piers escorted her to the door.

As he reached to open it, she said, "My lord, I cannot think the matter relevant, either to poor Claude's death or to the vandalism of the portrait. You have already achieved all we asked of you when you came. Leave the rest to the magistrate."

She smiled to show her friendship and gratitude, but her voice was firm and she did not quite meet his eyes.

"HOW DELICIOUS," HOPE said, his face alive with mockery. "What will you offer me not to tell Lady Haggard you are stealing from her dead guest?"

"Nothing," April said in deliberate surprise. She waved the paper contemptuously. "'Cause I ain't. Why'd anyone steal a scrap of paper?"

"Haven't you discovered what's inside it?"

"What?"

Hope came to a halt in front of her and leaned closer to whisper, "Opium."

April, who knew better than to get caught between him and the wardrobe, had already slid to one side and stepped away, as though examining the paper in the light from the window. "Opium? What's that then?"

He leaned one shoulder against the wardrobe, watching her like a cat preparing to pounce. "Sweet oblivion, my dear. Instead of pain, insomnia or sheer boredom. Want to try it?"

"Nah. Do you?"

"Not my thing. I prefer to remember my pleasures. Why are you snooping in here?"

"Lady Haggard asked me to look."

"Oh, please," Hope said in blatant disbelief.

"Well, she asked his lordship and I'm helping him. He'll be back in a shake."

His eyebrows lifted. "You're taking the opium for *him*? I'm surprised he knows about it."

"How come you do?"

"Oh, I know lots of things, my dear." He moved nearer her, but again she slipped just out of reach.

Torn between her instinct to bolt—she had a clear path to the door now—and her desire to find out what he knew, April chose the latter.

"Like what?" she said with a hint of derision. "That Mr. St. Etienne took powders for his headaches?"

"He didn't take them for headaches, my dear innocent," Hope said. "He took them because he had to. He was hopelessly dependent on the stuff. He couldn't get through the day without it."

"How d'you know that then?" she asked, allowing a hint of reluctant admiration into her voice.

"I told you. I know lots of things."

"You're making it up," she scoffed. "What d'you want to impress a servant for?"

He blinked, a hint of red creeping into his cheeks. But she seemed to have deprived him of words and lust at the same time. Avoiding her, he stalked straight to the door.

"Jumped up, common little trollop," he uttered, wrenching open the door so hard it almost hit the wall.

As he strode off along the passage, April almost laughed. *So that's how you knee gentlemen in the groin.*

All the same, her hand was not quite steady as she shoved the opium powder back in the black coat and closed the wardrobe door.

Lord Petteril strode in, a deep frown between his brows. "Did I see Randal Hope come out of here? Did he touch you?"

"Nah," April said, deliberately careless. "I got the measure of him now. He ain't as sure of himself as he looks."

"Ain't he?" Petteril murmured, his attention on the door as though gazing after Hope.

"Also, he says St. Etienne was lost to opium, dependent like. Do you believe that?"

Petteril's gaze came back to her. "I don't believe a man with a mushy brain painted that portrait of Haggs."

"Neither do I. But why'd he say that?"

"Maybe he believed it. The amount St. Etienne carried with him would certainly encourage the theory. But how would Hope know?"

"'Cause he's snooped before? 'Cause he got some from St. Etienne? Or maybe he saw him buy it. You don't get that much opium at a time from the nobs' apothecary shops. Maybe he came in to steal it—he was certainly quick enough to accuse *me*."

"Possibly," Petteril said in the peaceful voice he used if he didn't believe a word but didn't mind if you did. He sat down on the edge of the bed. "Lady Haggard knows of no one in the household or on the land who takes opium for pain or any other reason. She keeps a small bottle of laudanum in her medicine cabinet for emergencies."

April was disappointed. "Is that all?"

"No." He brushed at his thigh, as though removing a spec of dust from his immaculate pantaloons. It was a sign of discomfort. "Apparently my aunt took laudanum—I don't know to what degree—to help her sleep after my cousins died."

He didn't like his aunt. Neither did April—stupid, greedy old bat, happy to steal from Petteril and despise him at the same time. She had no understanding or appreciation of her nephew, and certainly no affection for him. Yet he did not want to explore her possible connection to St. Etienne. Perhaps because he didn't want to think about her grief or his own. So many of their family had died so quickly.

"Don't see her croaking St. Etienne for his opium though," April said. "Do you? If he was selling it, she'd just buy it. Or she'd send her maid to. Anyway, no one stole his opium. I don't see it being the reason he was murdered."

"She claims to be short of money, asking for an advance on her allowance." He sighed. "I need to talk to her. Did you find anything interesting?"

"Nothing. Not even a letter or any money to speak of." She brightened. "Here, do you suppose someone's prigged his stuff already?"

"Unlikely, but possible. Hope certainly didn't like St. Etienne."

"Prob'ly 'cause your Gussie was kind to him." She frowned. "What they invite Hope for anyway? He's too loose a screw for most of these people, ain't he?"

"I believe he was invited in the hope—if you'll pardon the pun—of entertaining..." He broke off, staring at her. "Why did he accept, though? As you say, not his kind of party, much too tame. And he had already accepted before my aunt did, so he didn't come because of Gussie."

April said, "I think he was like St. Etienne. He came because he was asked. Don't imagine he gets asked places often."

Slowly, she became aware of his unreadable gaze on her face. "What?" she demanded.

A quick half-smile dawned and vanished. "Nothing. It's a kind interpretation, but possibly a perceptive one." He stood and stretched his long, lean body. "I shall beard my aunt. See if you can talk to her maid—you know her, don't you?"

"Smithy."

On the way out, he took the key from the inside of the door and locked it on the outside before handing her the key. "Better give this to Yates or the housekeeper."

PIERS DISCOVERED HIS aunt and Gussie walking in the formal garden, escorted by Randal Hope. Only Gussie looked pleased to see him.

"Piers! Isn't it awful about poor Monsieur St. Etienne? Do you know what happened?"

"No more than you," Piers said apologetically.

Hope smirked, because he had Gussie on his arm and, no doubt, because he wanted Piers to believe he had enjoyed some intimacy with April in St. Etienne's bedchamber.

Aunt Hortensia, inevitably, sniffed. "I hope you have come to apologise to me."

"I *would* like a word," Piers said genially. "Why don't you walk ahead, Gussie? I'm sure Hope will protect you from snakes in the grass and all other threats."

Hope frowned as though trying to work out if there was an insult there, but Gussie, sparkling at Piers over her shoulder, was already dragging her escort onward.

"Well?" Aunt Hortensia demanded. "What new demands have you come to make?"

Piers sighed. He had no time and less inclination to quarrel. He longed for the peace of solitude and study and just occasional, congenial company. "I want to ask you about laudanum and opium."

"I am not an apothecary, Piers," she snapped.

"I am aware. Do you still take laudanum, Aunt?"

She stared at him, not answering.

He removed the dead head of a rose, mostly so he didn't have to look at her. "I did, for a time. At Oxford. It seemed to be the only way I could sleep. Trouble was, it gave me horrendous dreams. Did you find that?"

He risked a glance and saw her jaw dropping. She closed her mouth at once. "I don't recall," she said at last. "Nothing helped. Except my remaining children."

With difficulty, he focused on the matter in hand. "Then you have no need of it now for any pain or ailment?"

"No. Why should I?"

Clearly, the instant's softening was over. "As you say. What did you think of St. Etienne, Aunt?"

"That he was common and should not have been so constantly in-
flicted on Lady Haggard's gently born guests. But she made a pet of
him, and Augusta—as you know she is good-natured to a fault—followed her example."

His stomach jolted as though a boulder had landed in it. Dear God,
what if Gussie had not been flirting with Hope to make Haggs jealous, but with both of them to make St. Etienne jealous? Would St. Etienne have taken advantage of her, even while enjoying Irene Haggard's
favours? What if Aunt Hortensia had found out? In a protective rage,
was she not entirely capable of smacking him over the head with the
first thing that came to hand? The portrait of Sir Weston Haggard?

THE SERVANTS, NATURALLY, were shaken by the sudden death
in the house. Apart from anything else, servants were always the chief
suspects in any crime committed on the premises. And although they
didn't know for certain there had been a crime, they seemed to have a
sixth sense that suspected.

April kept coming across huddles of them, both upstairs and in the
servants' hall and kitchen. Entering the kitchen under pretence of seeking a late breakfast—she had been in too big a hurry to search St. Etienne's bedchamber to have eaten when Lord Petteril told her to—she
saw Smithy at once.

Lady Petteril must have made some effort to live within her means,
because she had brought only one maid to see to both her own needs
and her daughter's.

"There's only me now," Smithy had told April the other day. "She
dismissed her own dresser and kept me 'cause I'm cheaper."

Now Smithy was in the servants' hall with several other maids, including Mrs. Bramley's and a couple of the Pelton house maids. April,
her stomach rumbling, walked past the door and into the kitchen
where she begged some bread and cheese of the cook. Cook glared,

since she was busy with luncheon preparations, but cut her a thick slice of bread and sent her to the larder for cheese.

since she was busy with luncheon preparations, but cut her a thick slice of bread and sent her to the larder for cheese.

William was there on the same errand, and kindly cut her a generous hunk of cheese while getting his own.

"You're still here then," he noted roughly.

"His lordship brought me back. You misheard. I'm not working for Lady Haggs—I mean Haggard."

William glowered. "Wish you were."

"I don't. More interesting with 'is lordship."

William threw his bread and cheese onto the plate. "It's not right, April. All you've got's your reputation. Whatever he's told you, he'll never marry you."

April blinked, staring at him. He stared back, unexpectedly pale but grimly determined. She couldn't help it. She went off into a peel of laughter.

"Of course not," she scoffed. "You still think I'm his mistress—well I ain't. He wouldn't and neither would I. Even if I didn't work for him, he wouldn't look at me like that. You don't understand anything."

Although she stalked off with her bread and cheese, the novel idea that William was jealous struck her. He'd no bloody right, of course, but for some reason, it didn't make her angry, like his misjudgement of Petteril did. It was worth thinking about later. For now, she focused her mind on Smithy.

Mr. Yates was breaking up the servants' hall huddle, so April hastily attached herself to Smithy, who was the only one on a sanctioned break. Mr. Yates pursed his lips but left them to it.

"Your ladies upset, too?" April asked, by way of beginning a conversation. She took a bite of bread and cheese and realized how hungry she was. She'd got too used to regular meals.

"Well, you're expected to be miserable, aren't you?" Smithy said. "If you ask me, her ladyship's more annoyed about mourning getting in the way of entertainment than the poor Frenchman dying. Miss Gussie's got a kind heart, though. She cried." Smithy looked sad for a moment, then grinned. "Not that it'll hold her back for long."

"She's too used to death for so young a lady," April said wisely.

"Yes, but it's taught her to bounce back if nothing else."

"Is that what Lady Petteril learned too?"

Smithy sighed. "No. She learned to resent the world—or at least your Lord Petteril—and if you ever tell anyone I said that I'll—"

"'Course I wouldn't!" April interrupted, shocked. "How'd she get through the grief, then?" she asked after a moment. "Losing both sons and her husband so close together like that. Did she have doctors to help her?"

"Yes. Or they tried to."

April took another bite of her bread, chewed and swallowed. "I heard laudanum helps."

"I think they gave her some of that. Don't think it made much difference, though because the same bottle's still in the London house, more than half full, same as it was a year ago. She just seemed to remember she had other children and built her life around Miss Maria—that is Lady Gadsby—and Miss Augusta. And Mr. Bertie, to a lesser degree."

But not Lord Petteril, who was as much her nephew as Bertie. And had lost his own father and brother into the bargain. He'd had no one. April gazed at her bread and cheese, squashing her resentment.

"At least Lady Petteril didn't like Mr. St. Etienne, did she? 'Cause he was French, prob'ly, and the French killed one of her sons."

"Didn't help," Smithy allowed. "But he weren't a gentleman either. She was annoyed with Miss Augusta for being friendly to him. No point, is there? Miss Augusta's friendly to everyone. You going to eat all that cheese?"

April broke off a sizeable chunk and gave it to her. "Did he like her? I mean, did he keep the line?"

"I think Sir Peter would have flattened him if he didn't." Perhaps she saw the uncontrollable shock in April's face, for her jaw dropped in sudden realization of what she'd said. "Oh no, someone really flattened the poor b—Mr. St. Etienne?"

April shrugged. "Don't be daft," she managed.

But it couldn't be Haggs who'd hit St. Etienne, could it? He was Petteril's friend and a good man. Besides, gentlemen didn't murder their rivals. At the very worst, they fought duels.

On the other hand, St. Etienne hadn't been a gentleman by birth. And Haggs could have walloped him with the portrait in anger, not meaning to kill him...

But he'd admit it. To Lord Petteril if to no one else. No way would he lie to cover up what he'd done!

Or would he?

Chapter Thirteen

Luncheon was a somewhat subdued meal. The footmen serving all wore black armbands and the ladies wore their most sombre colours. On the other hand, luncheon was much less formal than the evening meal, and Piers was able to sit next to his cousin Gussie.

On her other side was Matthew Laughton, so Hope was reduced to sitting opposite her, between Mrs. Bramley and Marianne Orville. If Gussie noticed him, she gave no sign of it. She seemed most absorbed by Laughton's conversation.

Piers waited until, during a natural pause, Laughton turned to Lady Haggard and drew her into a discussion about poetry. Piers gave half his buttered roll to Gussie.

"What are you up to, coz?" he murmured. "Do you mean to have any of them?"

A delicate flush stole over Gussie's face. "I don't know what you mean," she said grandly.

"Yes, you do. It was a simple question."

"Then the simple answer is no."

"Then for whose benefit is all the flirting?"

She sighed and picked up the roll. "I hate you, Piers."

"No, you don't. Did you flirt with St. Etienne, too?"

"Barely at all."

"But you went to his studio sometimes. Was he going to paint you?"

She cast him a sceptical glance. "Can you imagine Mama allowing that?" She bit into the roll, using the time to think, then she added, "He did sketch me once, though. While I was talking to him."

"What did you talk about?"

"Nothing very much." A faint smile flickered as she returned to her soup. "Food. Faces. France, to name but three F's. He missed his home."

"Then he meant to go back when the war ends?"

"No, I don't think so. He said he was never going back."

"Why not?"

She shrugged. "I don't really know. Perhaps because he had lost everyone in France and no longer belonged there either." She cast him a direct glance, her eyes glistening suspiciously. "He was lonely."

And Gussie was kind, bless her. "Did he give you the sketch he made of you?"

She shook her head.

"And your visiting him in the studio—*did* it make any of your other swains jealous?"

"No, and I have no swains," she said grumpily.

Piers did not miss her dark, almost involuntary glance down the table at Haggs, who was helping Marianne to a slice of salmon. "Don't be so sure," he murmured. "And don't be in such a rush."

Her eyes widened, but again, her attention was claimed by Laughton and Piers turned back to his food, pausing only to return the amused smile of Jane Bramley across the table.

MATTHEW LAUGHTON WAS still furious with hurt because of his wife's quite disproportionate grief for the artist. But at least she behaved with dignity during luncheon and Laughton was almost consoled.

Until Lord Petteril stood up from the table, bowed to Lady Haggard and excused himself. Laughton refused to watch his departure, just because everyone else did. The viscount had a peculiarly elegant, loose-limbed stride that seemed to attract attention. Laughton curled his lip. The man was a tailor's manikin with untidy hair that no one had troubled to brush. A nonentity who, by a series of family misfortunes, had inherited his peerage by default without merit or suitability, let alone training.

And yet Susan watched him, a suddenly warm flash of speculation in her eyes.

Dear God, does it never end?

A few minutes later, the excruciating meal ended and they could all leave. This whole party, which he had expected to be merely dull, had turned into more of a nightmare. He needed to go for a long walk, or better still, ride, to exorcise his fury. Only it looked like rain outside, and he did not care to be soaked to the skin.

He strode off to the billiard room without so much as a glance at Susan. Hope was there already, which irritated him even more, though at least it was a distraction.

"Ah, good," said Hope, abandoning his shot and beginning to set up the balls for a game.

Laughton took a cue from the stand and chalked the end.

"I should suggest we play for money," Hope said. "You're far too angry to win. Has our noble viscount upset you?"

"I can't imagine why you would think so," Laughton snapped.

"Because I saw your wife watching him, too."

"Keep your eyes and you damned filthy—"

"Laughton, I'm on your side," Hope interrupted. "It's time someone taught Piers Withan a lesson."

Laughton looked at him. "What have you in mind?"

Hope placed the cue ball and bent over the table. "At school, he was never much of a fighter."

Smacked with Hope's cue, the white ball shot across the baize and smashed into the red balls, scattering them violently across the table.

"WHERE ARE HIS SKETCHES?" Piers said to April when she appeared in the studio in answer to his summons. He was crouching on the floor, raking through the little cupboard beneath the window seat, which contained a silver bell, a few small porcelain ornaments and a great many curtain hooks.

"What sketches?" April asked.

Piers pushed himself to his feet and closed the cupboard with his foot. "He made several of Haggs before he began painting. Apparently, he made at least one of Gussie, and I've seen him sketching outside."

April moved toward the desk where his slim sketchbook lay. "He did 'em in there, didn't he?"

"They've been torn out."

April rifled through the remaining empty pages. "So they have. By him? Or...?"

Or by whoever killed him. "I don't know. But if we can find them, they might provide some insight into who croaked him. At the moment, all we have is trivial motives. Does anyone kill for such silly reasons?"

"Yes," April said without hesitation. Life was cheap where she came from. "Though whether any of *these* people would is a different matter."

She rifled through the empty desk which contained nothing more than scented letter paper, a few pens and a bottle of ink. Piers knew because he had already looked.

"How many curtain hooks do they need?" he demanded, as he opened the cupboard beneath the third window seat.

April drifted across to St. Etienne's work chest. "Did you look in here?"

He glanced over his shoulder. "Yes. And there's no false bottom or hidden drawer beneath the obvious one." He frowned, rising to his feet once more.

April opened the chest and walked around it, her strong little fingers feeling around its walls and crevices on the outside. Her casualness was peculiarly studied as she asked, "Did Sir Peter get in a miff about his stepma and St. Etienne?"

"He didn't appear to. He is very understanding of human frailty. I should know."

"No one's good natured all the time," April said, her hands shifting over the lid of the chest, outside and in. "Has he got a temper?"

Piers considered, while her fingers glided inside the chest. She had small hands with long, slim fingers. Somehow, they had grown elegant. He said, "Haggs? Not that he can't control. But you know when he is angry."

She leaned back, peering at each side of the chest.

"Lady Haggard's confession did not make him angry," Piers said, raising his gaze to her face. "He loved his father but he never hero-worshipped him as Orville did, or all these women. He would not kill a man for an *affaire* with her, not if she was willing."

April's fingers stilled, though she didn't look up from the chest. "What about for an affair with Miss Gussie?"

That swiped the breath from his body so fast that he dropped into the chair. April cast him a quick glance and returned to the chest, running her finger along the rim at the back, just under the hinges of the lid.

"St. Etienne was not having an affair with Gussie," he said firmly. "She felt sorry for him."

"Maybe, but did Haggs know that? I mean Sir Peter."

"I imagine so. What are you doing?"

"The back's too thick," April said.

He sprang out of the chair, just as she grinned. "Aha!"

A length of wood along the back rim of the box moved and she slid it right out.

"Oh, well done," he breathed.

Flushing slightly at the praise, she drew out a large sheet of paper, and then a wad of others. She dropped to the floor and began to spread them out.

There were two of Haggs, one in a pose like the finished portrait, the other a close study of his expressive face. Unexpectedly, one was of Piers. He didn't recognize it for a moment, until April gave a little crow of pleasure and reached for it. There was a sketch of a hand holding a paintbrush, including every wrinkle of the skin, every vein, and on the same page a cloud-shaped lump filled with a mass of thin, curling tubes. He hadn't appeared to like the latter for he had scribbled over it.

"What's that?" April asked.

"A brain," said Piers, who had been friends with several students of medicine. "Or at least an impression of one. And there is Gussie."

The sketch showed all her liveliness, the sparkle of her personality, and yet it was the picture of a child, not a woman.

"That is how he thought of her," Piers said, picking it up.

"And that's how he thought of Lady H." April pointed at the two sketches of Lady Haggard, one of her noble profile, one of her gazing straight out, her smile curiously aware and very womanly. "Good, weren't he?"

She grinned at the rest that were almost caricatures of the other guests, haughty and disapproving or self-righteous, nostrils flaring like Orville or decadently sneering like Hope. Aunt Hortensia appeared to be sniffing, the small mole at the corner of her mouth stretched as she pursed her lips.

Piers grinned too. "No wonder he hid them."

"Will I put them back?"

Piers hesitated. "For now. He has no kin that we know of. We should leave them with Lady Haggard."

April gathered them up and sat back on her heels. "What now?"

"Collect Haggs and go and hassle the doctor."

"There's none of Miss Orville or the Laughtons or Mrs. Bramley," April noted. "Wonder what that means."

"That they didn't interest him, probably. He had already painted the Laughtons."

"Do you think he loved Lady H?"

Piers glanced at her in some surprise. "In his own way. I suspect he loved art more."

"Fair. She prob'ly loved Sir Weston more. Will I fetch my cloak?"

SINCE RAIN WAS THREATENING, Haggs ordered the carriage and they set off toward Pelton village.

"Thanks for coming with us," Piers said to Haggs. "I need you to smooth the way or he might not tell us anything."

"My pleasure," Haggs said sardonically. "I'm just glad to be out of the house for a while. I find I'm looking at everybody differently, wondering how and why they might have murdered St. Etienne. I don't suppose you have any ideas?"

"None that have evidence to support them. None that even feel right."

"Then you don't believe my cousin Kenneth is a murderer as well as a vandal?"

"Not really," Piers said with a sigh.

"It's going to be an almighty scandal," Haggs said gloomily. "Whatever happens."

"Your guests have made no effort to flee?"

"Not apart from Kenneth, who must now leave early tomorrow for church. He has put it off for today." He stirred. "There must be rumours, of course, but we did not tell anyone the truth about St. Etienne. We merely said he had died suddenly."

"Anything else will keep until we *know* the truth," Piers said.

"If we ever do."

The carriage rumbled on. April was scribbling in her book, apparently uninhibited by the lurching of the vehicle.

Piers said, "Are you satisfied that Orville vandalized the portrait?"

"I don't understand it," Haggs replied after a moment. "But I see no reason for him to lie about it."

"Who would he cover for?"

"Marianne, I suppose. Possibly Irene and me, but he has confessed to us both."

Marianne had rather slipped beneath Piers's notice. He suspected she did that rather a lot and wondered if it were deliberate.

"No," Haggs said, watching him. "I don't believe Marianne vandalized my father's portrait. And I certainly don't think she bashed St. Etienne over the head with it."

Piers sighed. "Fair enough."

Dr. Roberston occupied a comfortable looking house near the village green, more substantial than a cottage but hardly the abode of a wealthy man. Haggs led the way through the garden gate and up the neat path to the painted front door with its well-polished brasses.

They were admitted by a plump, comfortable lady whom Haggs introduced as Mrs. Robertson.

She beamed at them. "Come in, come in! I'll tell Cyril you're here. What a relief you're not patients! I imagine," she added with sudden doubt. Bustling forward to a front parlour, she confided over her shoulder. "He's in the basement. More of a cellar, really, it's so cold. It's where he does his autopsies and his tests. Take a seat, sirs." Her glance fell doubtfully on April, as though wondering what to do with her.

"I'll stand," April assured her.

Mrs. Robertson hurried off. Piers could hear her feet clattering on wooden steps, then a great thump of a knock as she yelled, "Cyril! Sir Peter's here with another gentleman! You'd better come up!"

Piers could not make out the answer, but it was two sets of feet that crashed back up the same staircase. A few seconds later, Mrs. Robertson stuck her head around the door. "He's just washing his hands and will be with you directly. I'll set Lizzie on to fetch tea!"

They did not have long to wait before another quick tread sounded in the passage and Dr. Robertson strode in, still buttoning his coat.

"My lord. Sir Peter," he said briskly, shaking hands with each. He glanced at April, blinked and then turned back to the men. "To what do I owe the honour? No one is ill at Pelton Park?"

"No, no," Haggs said easily. "I realize we have given you very little time, but you'll understand it is of vital importance to me to know what happened to St. Etienne."

"My report to the magistrate is not yet ready."

Haggs held his gaze until a reluctant smile dawned on the doctor's face. "Sit," he said ruefully.

April got out her notebook and pencil and slid down the wall to sit on the floor and rest the book on her knee. Robertson, who sat with his back to her, did not notice.

"The head injury did not kill him," he said bluntly. "It was not severe enough and damaged nothing vital. I have examined his brain."

Piers blinked to dispel the image of a bodiless brain being dissected by his medical friend. He swallowed.

"And it was not damaged?" Haggs said eagerly.

"Oh, it is damaged, but not by the blow. Rather by the unkindness of nature—or God, if you prefer. He had a growth, a large tumour, on his brain."

In the stunned silence, Piers's own brain reached for understanding.

"Explains the 'eadaches and the opium," April said.

Dr. Robertson's head whipped round. "Opium?"

Piers extracted the powder from his pocket and leaned forward to pass it to Robertson. "He took these whenever headaches became unbearable. He had a lot of it in his room."

"I found some in his stomach, too," the doctor said.

"Enough to have killed him?" Piers asked.

Robertson frowned at him. "I would not have said so, no, but—"

"Then the tumour killed him?"

"It was advanced," Robertson said.

"And yet he expected to live," Piers said, "if he had all that opium."

"By the size of the tumour, I would have expected him to deteriorate, but to live another few months. But sometimes the body has just had enough. To be frank, it was a blessing for him."

Silence fell.

Haggs said what they must all have been thinking. "Yet someone hated him enough to break my father's portrait over his head."

"An unnecessarily vile act of hatred," Robertson said. "I'm sorry."

"Could the shock of the blow to his head have determined the time of his death?" Piers asked.

Robertson shrugged helplessly. "It's possible. I still think he was dead already, though probably not for long."

Then, did it really matter who hit him? On the doctor's testimony, the law was unlikely to prosecute anyone of importance for a lesser crime like damaging a corpse.

An unnecessarily vile act of hatred. Who would want such a perpetrator as a guest in their house?

It was all wrong.

Piers sprang to his feet. He needed to leave, to think.

But Mrs. Robertson sailed into the room with a tray full of tea things and he felt obliged to take the heavy tray from her and then stay for tea.

Mrs. Robertson, enchanted that a lord should be so considerate to her, did not appear to even notice April, sitting on her parlour floor, her back against the wall.

Piers gulped his tea, scalding his throat, all but twitching with tension. Distracted by the whirling thoughts and puzzle pieces that would not quite come together, he dropped a scone into his pocket.

He bit his tongue as long as he could, then, set his cup and saucer on the table before jumping to his feet once more.

"Thank you for the tea, ma'am. Delicious scones. Doctor, I'm grateful for your time and your information."

Haggs, halfway through a sandwich, blinked at him in surprise, but there was nothing he could do except abandon his plate and his cup and follow Piers, thanking both Robertsons as he went.

Only when they were in the carriage once more, did he aim a clout at Piers's head. "I'm starving, you selfish—"

"Sorry," Piers said. He delved into his pocket, took out the slightly fluffy scone, and dusted it off before passing it to April.

She took it with a grin and bit into it at once.

"What?" Piers said, becoming aware of Haggs's open-mouthed stare. "She didn't get any."

Chapter Fourteen

As soon as the carriage came to a halt outside the door of Pelton House, Piers leapt out and strode away across the lawn.

"Good afternoon, Withy," Haggs called after him sardonically.

Piers spared him no more than a glance over his shoulder. Haggs spread his arms outward in enquiry. April, who always seemed to understand his need for solitude, was already hurrying away toward the servants' door. Piers walked on, going over everything in his head from the moment he had first seen the vandalized portrait of Sir Weston. Thinking, after all, was what he did best.

Thinking... Had St. Etienne's tumour interfered with his ability to think? Had he damaged the portrait himself and then forgotten? In which case, why would Orville have taken the blame for him? Compassion? Christian charity?

Piers could not see it. Orville was much more rigid. He disliked Frenchmen and artists, and he worshipped Sir Weston. Besides, his shame had seemed genuine. And judging by the artist's final work, St. Etienne's illness certainly had not interfered with his skill, or the larger implications that seemed to flow from it.

Vaguely aware of other people in the distance, Piers veered away from them and into the wood, still deep in thought and memory. He would have to try and discover where everyone was in those few hours between the time Lady Haggard had last seen St. Etienne and the moment Piers had found his body. Judging by his previous attempt to locate everyone on the night of the portrait's defacement, that would not be easy.

Why in hell hit a man who is already dead?

Because your hatred is so intense. Or because you don't know he is dead.

From his appearance when Piers had walked into the studio that morning, St. Etienne could have been asleep in the chair. Whoever hit him could have thought so, too. After all, his eyes were closed...although they tended to open at death, did they not? Just as April said.

A twig broke close by. He could hear the brush of clothing against undergrowth. Again, he veered away from it, too deep in thought even to be irritated. Somehow, it was important that St. Etienne's eyes were closed. He was reaching for why, when Matthew Laughton stepped through the trees into his path.

Piers nodded curtly by way of greeting and would have passed on, except that Laughton didn't move.

"A little rude of you, my lord," he sneered. "Are you in so much of a hurry to reach your assignation? Perhaps I should accompany you."

"Excuse me," Piers said vaguely, stepping around him. "I'll talk to you later."

Laughton seized his arm, stopping him in his tracks so suddenly that he stumbled. "Your sheer gall is incredible!"

Looking at him in faint surprise, Piers finally registered the pure fury of the man, and frowned.

"What is it?" he asked. Had Laughton been the one who snapped and in a jealous rage hit his wife's former lover with one of his own paintings while he was asleep? Surely Laughton was the type who would want his victim to know.

Laughton pulled back his clenched fist. "You will stay away from my wife!"

As the fist flew at his face, Piers ducked. "I will," he said, as the force of the missed punch sent Laughton crashing into him. Braced, Piers caught him and heaved him upright, which only seemed to infuriate him further.

"*I will?*" he repeated, incredulously. "That is not enough! You, my lord, need a sound thrashing!"

The words triggered a sudden memory. School. Randal Hope was always threatening sound thrashings.

"Of course," Piers said. "Hope put you up to this, didn't he? He's always been good at getting other people to do his work for him."

"You should know," Hope sneered, stepping out of the undergrowth so that they stood one on either side of him. "You did enough of mine."

Piers had had enough. "And you were too stupid even to know why. Good afternoon."

He bent and swiped up his hat which had fallen off when he ducked. But Hope, seeing him at a disadvantage, hurled himself on his back, shoving him to the ground.

It was ridiculously like a playground tussle, with more rolling and pushing than hits. At least until Piers, temporarily on his back, saw Laughton's boot aimed at his ribs. Piers grabbed the foot and twisted, and Laughton fell, howling.

Piers, just because he was larger, rolled Hope under him and sat on him, grabbing both his hands and bearing them to the ground. Hope roared with fury, straining and bucking his body but Piers held on grimly, glad of the extra strength in his arms produced by so much riding and driving in the last few months.

Hope squeezed his eyes shut, working up a final effort to dislodge Piers.

Eyes. Someone shut his eyes.

And he knew who.

Abruptly, he let go of Hope and jumped to his feet. Hope and Laughton were so stunned, they just stared at him.

"Later," he threw vaguely over his shoulder and almost burst his way out of the woods. At the last moment, he remembered to pick up his hat. Again.

A FOOTMAN LET HIM IN the front door. He was very tall and broad of shoulder, and it struck Piers that this might well be April's William. He paused and peered at him. The youth had been trained to keep his face expressionless, but there was a definite hostility in his eyes.

This pleased Piers rather than offended him, so he thanked the man as he handed over his hat. "Er... Perhaps someone could give it a bit of a brush? It had an accident in the woods."

Without waiting to hear the answer, Piers strode to the studio, rattled the handle, and then remembered that it was kept locked and he had the key. Fishing it out of his pocket, he unlocked the door and went in.

Striding straight to the artist's work chest, he opened it and searched out the secret slide. He was too impatient and so it took twice as long as it should have, but eventually, he had the cover off and extracted the sketches from it. He rifled through them until he found the one of the brain.

Unlike the hand on the same page, the brain was not an accurate drawing but a mere impression. When he had first looked at it, Piers had thought it must have displeased St. Etienne, because he'd scribbled over some of it. Now, gazing at it with a different understanding, he perceived that the scribble was almost solid, a part of the impression. The scribbled area was a growth, a tumour.

"I will paint you next if there is time," St. Etienne had said to Piers.

"He new he was ill," Piers muttered. "He knew he would die."

"Who did?" April said, wandering in. "St. Etienne?"

"Yes." He dropped the sketches on the table beside the chest and most of them slid onto the floor. "Tidy them up, will you? I have to see Lady Haggard."

"No, wait, mister!" she called in frustration as he swept past her. "What have you found out? You *know*, don't you?"

He knew. And it hurt his heart.

WHEN HE KNOCKED ON her sitting room door, it was Lady Haggard's voice that bade him enter. Deal must have been about her duties elsewhere. But when he walked in, he was disconcerted to find Haggs with her.

"Good Lord," she said, gazing at Piers in some amusement. "Have you been rolling in the mud?"

"Yes." Piers glanced down at his fawn breeches, stained with earth and grass, and his coat which still had bits of twig attached. God knew what state his face was in. Despite his urgency, he blushed. "Sorry. I shall change directly, but I'm afraid it's important that I speak to you. Haggs, could you give me a few minutes privacy with her ladyship?"

Haggs frowned, though he would probably have gone had his stepmother not seized his arm.

"There is no need for Peter to go," she said haughtily. "I have nothing to hide from him."

But her eyes were frightened, and Piers knew he was right.

Damn. This had never been so difficult before.

Regally, she seated herself, her armchair like a throne, and met his gaze. Haggs stood beside her like a knight protector.

Piers swallowed. He did not sit. "My lady, were you aware that St. Etienne was ill?"

"Again, I knew about his migraines," she said with exaggerated patience. "I already told you he took opium occasionally to relieve the pain."

"But you knew it was not mere migraines. You knew he had a tumour on his brain. You knew he was dying."

Her eyelids fluttered, as though she would close her eyes, but she didn't. She held his gaze and Piers could only admire her courage.

"Before the magistrate comes," Piers said slowly, "I would be grateful if you explained why you broke your husband's portrait over St. Etienne's head."

LEFT IN THE STUDIO, impatient to know the truth and angry he
had not told her first, April gathered up the fallen sketches and replaced
them in their hidden compartment inside the chest. But as she picked
up the sliding cover, she paused, then laid it down again. Delving back
into the compartment, she rifled the drawings until she found the one
of Lord Petteril. She removed it and after only a quick glance, she rolled
it up and placed it inside the bag at her waist. It only just fitted.

She closed the chest and wandered over to the window. Mr.
Laughton was limping across the lawn toward the front door, his
clothes streaked with mud. Beside him was Randal Hope, in much the
same condition only without the limp. They were both scowling.

She suddenly remembered the dirt on Petteril's clothes—and on
his hands and face. Had he been *fighting* with those two?

Petteril never chose a fight, but she knew from experience that he
was oddly capable when one was forced upon him. Because he fought
with his head more than his fists. And these two, especially Hope, had
the air of bullies. She hoped Petteril had drawn their corks, though she
doubted it since she could see no blood. Perhaps it was more visible
close up. One could dream.

Suddenly, she hated this house and just about everyone in it. Well,
the mystery was solved and they would be leaving, thank God.

Spinning on her heel, she stamped out of the room and across the
hall to the baize door and the servants' stairs. She reached the attic un-
challenged and barged into the room she shared with Deal. Who, she
acknowledged, had been very good about sharing, although no doubt
she would be glad to have her chamber to herself again.

So would April. Scrabbling under the narrow bed, she pulled out
her empty travelling bag and dropped it on the coverlet. Hastily, she
threw in her hairbrush and face cloth and soap. She added her boots,
her spare dresses and caps, night rail and chemises. Then, checking first

that the door was closed, she removed St. Etienne's sketch of Petteril and put it in the bag, covering it up with the clothes.

That felt better. With satisfaction, she placed her packed bag back under the bed and hurried back downstairs to the studio to wait for Lord Petteril.

"DAMN IT, WITHY, HAVE *you* had a knock on the head?" Haggs said furiously. "You owe Irene an apology!"

"Perhaps," Piers said steadily, "but I would like to hear it from Lady Haggard."

His gaze had never left hers and she continued to hold it. For a moment, it seemed she would not budge. And then she whispered, "I did not kill him."

Haggs, his fists clenched, advanced on Piers, who kept his attention still on Lady Haggard.

"I know," Piers said.

"Then what the devil do you mean throwing such vile accusations at her?" Haggs demanded.

"Peter, please," she said wearily. "I did not kill Claude St. Etienne."

Piers said gently, "When you found him, he was already dead, wasn't he?"

She nodded. A tear trickled from the corner of her eye. "You are right. He was dying of a growth on his brain. He thought he had a few months to live, but he knew the pain would only get worse. I obtained the opium for him."

"When?" Piers asked.

She waved one impatient hand. "Last week? Shortly after he arrived at Pelton, at any rate. I had my man of business arrange for it to be sent from London, pretending I had a dying servant in my care. It seemed to help Claude."

She dashed the back of her hand over her wet cheek. "He no longer feared the pain, just that the growth might affect his thinking, his painting. He feared that more than anything, was desperate to produce his masterpiece and furious that the only way he could live was painting dull portraits of the rich and smug, none of which inspired him."

Haggs had stopped glaring at Piers and sat down too quickly. "No one killed him? As the doctor said, he died of the tumour?"

"I believe so," Piers said. "It's almost as if...having finished your portrait, he knew he had his masterpiece and could give up. I don't know, but I am glad that he finished it and that it is as it is."

"So am I," Lady Haggard said, wiping her eyes again.

"Will you tell us what happened?" Piers said.

Irene Haggard swallowed and closed her eyes. "I went to see him in the studio that evening, and just as I entered, the pain hit him, far worse than it had ever been. I gave him some wine, with an opium powder, and after a little, the pain lessened again. He smiled at me and showed me the portrait."

She gasped. "He was so proud of it! And it is magnificent, is it not?"

"Even I think so," Haggs said, a catch in his voice. "And I hate looking at myself."

"Something suddenly struck a chord in him," Lady Haggard said. "I don't know whether it was when he studied your face in a particular moment or if it only happened after he began to paint, but suddenly he saw the nobility in you, in all of us, as though the chip had suddenly fallen from his shoulder, taking all his resentments and unhappiness with it."

She drew in an unsteady breath. "I congratulated him and he bade me leave him to clear up and to compose himself. So I did. He was so contented, so serene. I waited and waited for him, long after midnight. I did not want to constrict him, but I knew I would never sleep until I saw he was still well.

"So I rose and went downstairs once more. The lights were all on in the studio and he sat in that chair." She pointed to the wooden chair where Piers had found him. "He had tidied up as he said he would. Peter's portrait was drying on the easel, his brushes were cleaned and away, as were his paints, his palette." She gasped again. "I thought he was asleep, except..."

She shook her head, unable to say the words.

"Except his eyes were open," Piers said. "You closed them."

She nodded. "He had no breath, no heartbeat, no pulse. I knew he was dead. And yet he should have had longer."

"You opened the window?" Piers asked.

She nodded.

"Why?" Haggs asked helplessly.

She shook her head, burying her face in her hands.

"Because she was afraid he had taken his own life," Piers said. "She was afraid he had swallowed a few more of all these powders she had acquired for him, because he knew he was failing and could not face the weeks of pain to come. To say nothing of the damage to his mind."

Lady Haggard scrubbed her fingers over her face and into her hair. "I thought he had chosen to end his life at this high point, having completed his beautiful portrait."

"A suicide is deprived of a Christian burial," Piers said. "He is shamed and reviled when he cannot defend himself. He should be pitied, but outwardly at least, he is not. Not in his own Church and not in ours. So you opened the windows to make it look as if a stranger had entered the house. And you hit him with Sir Weston's portrait."

"I did," she whispered.

"Why?" Haggs demanded. "Why my father's portrait?"

"Oh God, I don't know. Because it was there. Because Piers had told me Susan Laughton was not guilty of the vandalism so I knew she would not be blamed. I hoped this would look as if the same stranger who had defaced it had come back and murdered him. And of course, no murderer would ever be found, since there had been no murder. I didn't know Kenneth had already confessed to Piers."

"Or that St. Etienne had not killed himself, but merely succumbed to his illness," Piers said. "I am sorry."

For a moment no one spoke, and Piers turned to leave.

Haggs' voice stayed him. "Then Kenneth really did damage the portrait?"

Piers nodded. "The crimes were not related at all. In fact, in the case of St. Etienne's death, I do not believe there has been any crime, merely an excess of compassion and care."

Lady Haggard began to cry again. Haggs looked at her helplessly, then said, "Will the magistrate see it that way?"

"If you tell it properly. St. Etienne died of natural causes. Dr. Robertson will confirm that. You may easily imply a servant—a guest's servant would be best, naming no names, of course—bore a grudge against him and whacked him when he thought he was asleep. The servant has been punished and dismissed and already fled to London."

Haggs regarded him with some awe. "Occasionally, Withy, you scare me."

"Piers." It was the first time Lady Haggard had used his name since he arrived. She flung out her hand and he went to her quickly, clasping her trembling fingers. "Thank you," she whispered. "I'm so sorry I misled you. I thought I had to."

"I know."

"You should have trusted him," Haggs said severely. "And me."

"I know." She gave Haggs her other hand and smiled somewhat shakily. "You are good boys."

Piers kissed her hand and got out. Emotional scenes were too damned difficult.

Chapter Fifteen

"So what now?" April asked in the studio, once Lord Petteril had told her everything, and she had marvelled at his cleverness in working it out.

"Now," he said, rising and indicating she should precede him, "we go to Sillitrees."

"Today?" she asked eagerly.

"If you can be ready to go in an hour with all your goodbyes said, we should be there before dark."

"I can be ready in five minutes!" She ran out of the door, and all but skipped across the hall to the baize door.

In no time, she was in the kitchen, traveling cloak around her shoulders, carpet bag in hand.

"You're going," Cook observed with a nod. "We'll miss you. Didn't expect to, but there it is."

April laughed. "Where's Miss Deal?"

"With her ladyship. She's still a bit upset about the foreign gent, but there, you can't help where you die, can you?"

"Not usually," April said cheerfully. "Will you say goodbye to Miss Deal for me? Tell her I'm very grateful for her kindness and I learned a lot."

"Bless you, so I will," Cook said, beaming. "Get away with you and come back soon."

April grinned and surged off to the kitchen door. Here, she encountered William, who must have been waiting for her.

"So, you're off," he said aggressively. "And glad of it, I see."

"Only 'cause I won't have to look at your disapproving mug any more."

His face softened. "I don't disapprove. I like you."

April shifted to the other foot, feeling heat seep up her neck and into her face. "You're not so very bad yourself," she muttered.

"Then you'll miss me?" he asked.

"Nah. Well, maybe the *tiniest* bit."

He grinned and kissed her cheek before she could dodge it.

"Get off!" She stepped back out of his reach, now blushing furiously.

"See you when you come back then," he said.

April laughed. "Not if I see you first!"

To the sound of his laughter, she bolted out the back door. Oddly, she wasn't unhappy. She hadn't cringed when he came near her. He was a good lad and he liked her. This didn't displease her. Admiration made you feel good.

Probably, it made Lord Petteril feel good too. Miss Austen's admiration. Mrs. Bramley's. That made it more bearable.

She turned the corner to the stable yard and as if she'd conjured the woman by her thought, she saw Mrs. Bramley walking toward her with Petteril. He must have been ordering the horses put to the curricle, for the grooms were leading out the greys and getting them into harness.

Before they could see her, April bolted behind the old tack room shed and waited for Petteril and Mrs. Bramley to pass.

"You are going so soon," Mrs. Bramley said sadly.

"I did not mean to stop at Pelton at all," Petteril replied. "I'm glad I did."

Mrs. Bramley walked past, taking his lordship's arm with, April thought, far too proprietorial a manner. "So am I. And I'm glad we did not give in to temptation."

"Then so am I," Petteril said.

They paused a moment, perhaps because Mrs. Bramley was holding him back. "If it had been anyone," she said softly, "it would have been you."

Petteril bent and kissed her cheek, much as William had kissed April's a few minutes ago. "Likewise," he said. "Goodbye, Jane. I wish you all the joy in the world."

He strode away toward the house alone. Mrs. Bramley raised her gloved hand to her cheek for a moment, then smiled tremulously, straightened her back and strolled on in his wake.

April leaned her head back against the wall. She found she was smiling. Because he hadn't taken Mrs. Bramley to his bed after all.

Not that it made a blind bit of difference to April. But feelings seemed to go their own way, without reference to the brain. She walked out to pet the greys and chat to the grooms while she waited for Lord Petteril.

ON THE STAIRCASE, PIERS almost ran into Matthew Laughton.

Like Piers, he had changed his clothes. Unlike Piers, who had too many other things on his mind, his face flamed. He looked as if he didn't know whether to be angry or ashamed, and then decided simply to run past.

It was Piers who stood in his way.

"A word," Piers said low. "For whatever you judge that word is worth, I have never touched your wife nor made any plans to. She has given no sign whatever that any such would be acceptable."

"I've seen you looking. I've seen *her*."

A faint smile twisted Piers's lips. "Everyone *looks*, Laughton. Don't you?"

Piers ran on up the stairs, feeling Laughton's puzzled stare boring into his back. Then he must have seen his wife because he said hoarsely, "Susan."

"Oh, Matthew, shall we go home?" she said, her voice muffled as if in his shoulder.

Piers smiled to himself at the top of the stairs and strode along the landing to his bedchamber.

Stewart, his valet, would no doubt be shocked by Piers's packing method, which was simply to hurl everything into the same, capacious bag. He did not have a great deal of kit with him since he'd sent most of it to Sillitrees with Stewart already.

Closing the bag, he glanced around the room to make sure he had not forgotten anything. April's letter of resignation glared at him from the mantelpiece.

Slowly, he walked over and picked it up. Curiosity was fierce. So was longing. And the knowledge that the truth, whatever of it she had written, might help him. And she would never know. It would hardly be the first thing he had hidden from her.

His lips twisted. His finger slid under the fold and halted.

She had asked him to burn it. She trusted him.

A sudden wave of happiness swept over him. She *trusted* him, even if only not to read her damned letter of resignation and to burn it as she had requested. To live up to that was the least he could do.

He dropped the letter into the grate, then fetched the flint and struck a spark. He watched the letter curl into the flames.

Then he turned, picked up his bag and went out to join April.

Watch out for Book 5

Petteril's Wife (Lord Petteril Mysteries, 5), coming spring 2024!
Here's a sneak peek.

"COR," SAID PIERS WITHAN, Viscount Petteril.

It was hardly his usual expression of awe but the sight of Lisbon
from the River Tagus seemed to merit something special. A beautiful,
white-washed city rose grandly up from the water's edge, spilling over
several hills into the distance, elegant domes and spires reaching up into a sky of unchanging blue. The sheer loveliness took his breath away.

Beside him at the ship rail, his assistant April nudged his elbow. "I
believe you need to adjust your language, Mr. Whittey. Unless we are
swapping places."

"You are quite correct, Mrs. Whittey," he replied, dragging his gaze
from the city to her no less beautiful face. Her golden fair hair was el-
egantly pinned behind her head, a wide-brimmed straw hat with blue
feathers and ribbons, tipped forward over his face to shade her com-
plexion from the hot sun. Her blue eyes, however, danced with mischief, making his lips twitch. "Although it might be fun."

"Swapping places?" she asked with a quick grin. "Can we?"

"Not this time," he said with some regret. "We have a serious task
ahead of us."

April turned back to face Lisbon. "Have you ever seen anywhere
more beautiful?"

"I don't believe I have."

"You'll change your mind quick enough when we get ashore," said
their fellow passenger, Lieutenant Roberts, grinning with a hint of pity
at their naivety. He, returning from England after medical treatment,
had passed through Lisbon twice before.

"Never, sir," April said fervently.

She carried off this masquerade as a lady perfectly. No one would have guessed from her confident posture that she had never worn such fine clothes before, or from her speech that she had grown up on the back streets of London docks and St. Giles. She had always been an excellent mimic and by now, since Piers made her keep the accent even when they were alone, she hardly ever slipped. The occasional word of thieves' cant had occasionally popped out, but in refined tones and fortunately not in the presence of anyone who understood.

Piers was both amused and delighted. He did not allow himself to analyse that delight too closely, contenting himself with acknowledging its usefulness in the task ahead.

Lisbon only grew more beautiful the nearer they sailed.

"If I was Major Withan," April whispered, "I'd lose myself here too and never leave."

Piers didn't put it past his hedonistic cousin Bertie, except that desertion from the army was seriously dishonourable and Bertie rather needed the adulation of his peers. Piers wished he was here merely for pleasure, but perhaps there would be time later...

The harbour, where warships bumped shoulders with trading vessels, was bustling with activity and colour. Cargoes were loaded and unloaded amidst multi-lingual shouting. Soldiers in reds and blues and greens flowed off ships into the organized chaos of the quay.

But it was not just the light and bright clothing that fascinated Piers. Under the blazing sun, with April's hand in his arm, pinching and wriggling against his sleeve in excitement, he walked off the ship and up the steps onto dry land and into an enchantingly foreign country.

READ THE REST IN PETTERIL'S Wife, coming spring 2024.

About the Author

Mary Lancaster is a USA Today bestselling author of award winning historical romance and historical fiction. She lives in Scotland
with her husband, one of three grown-up kids, and a small dog with a
big personality.

Her first literary love was historical fiction, a genre which she rel-
ishes mixing up with romance and adventure in her own writing. Several of her novels feature actual historical characters as diverse as Hungar-
ian revolutionaries, medieval English outlaws, and a family of eternally
rebellious royal Scots. To say nothing of Vlad the Impaler.

More recently, she has enjoyed writing light, fun Regency ro-
mances, with occasional forays into the Victorian era. With its slight
change of emphasis, *Petteril's Thief*, was her first Regency-set historical
mystery.

CONNECT WITH MARY ON-line – she loves to hear from readers:

Email Mary: Mary@MaryLancaster.com

Website: http://www.MaryLancaster.com

Newsletter sign-up: https://marylancaster.com/newsletter/

Facebook: https://www.facebook.com/mary.lancaster.1656

Facebook Author Page: https://www.facebook.com/MaryLancasterNovelist/

Twitter: @MaryLancNovels https://twitter.com/MaryLancNovels

Bookbub: https://www.bookbub.com/profile/mary-lancaster

Printed in Great Britain
by Amazon